THE
KILLER'S
TEARS

THE KILLER'S TEARS

Anne-Laure Bondoux

Les Larmes de l'Assassin
Translated from the French by
Y. Maudet

DELACORTE PRESS

Published by
Delacorte Press
an imprint of
Random House Children's Books
a division of Random House, Inc.
New York

Originally published in France in 2003 by Bayard Editions Jeunesse

Visit us on the Web! www.randomhouse.com/teens
Educators and librarians, for a variety of teaching tools, visit us at
www.randomhouse.com/teachers

Library of Congress Cataloging-in-Publication Data

Bondoux, Anne-Laure.
[Larmes de l'assassin. English]
The killer's tears / Anne-Laure Bondoux ; translated from the French by Y. Maudet.
p. cm.
Originally published in France in 2003 by Bayard Editions Jeunesse under the title: Les
larmes de l'assassin.
Summary: A young boy, Paolo, and the man who murdered his parents, Angel, gradually
become like father and son as they live and work together on the remote Chilean farm
where Paolo was born.
ISBN 0-385-73293-7 (trade) — ISBN 0-385-90314-6 (glb)
[1. Fathers and sons—Fiction. 2. Metamorphosis—Fiction. 3. Interpersonal relations—
Fiction. 4. Robbers and outlaws—Fiction. 5. Chile—Fiction.] I. Maudet, Y. II. Title.
PZ7.B63696Ki 2006
[Fic]—dc22   2005008845

The text of this book is set in 12-point Goudy.

Book design by Kenny Holcomb

Printed in the United States of America

February 2006

10 9 8 7 6 5 4 3 2

BVG

Area Enlarged

BOLIVIA

PARAGUAY

ARGENTINA

BRAZIL

URUGUAY

Valparaiso

SANTIAGO

BUENOS AIRES

A
N
D
E
S

M
O
U
N
T
A
I
N
S

Talcahuano

Temuco

CHILE

P
A
C
I
F
I
C

O
C
E
A
N

P
A
M
P
A
S

A
T
L
A
N
T
I
C

O
C
E
A
N

P
A
T
A
G
O
N
I
A

SOUTH
AMERICA

0   100   200
Scale of Miles

Puerto Natales

Strait of Magellan

Strait of Magellan

Punta Arenas

N

CHAPTER ONE

NO ONE EVER arrived here by chance. Here was nearly the end of the world, close to the southernmost tip of Chile, which resembles lace in the cold Pacific waters.

On this land, everything was so tough, desolate, and abused by the wind that even the stones seemed in pain. Yet just before the desert and the sea, a narrow, gray-walled structure emerged from the ground: the Poloverdo farm.

Travelers who reached this point were surprised to find a house. They would walk down the path and knock on the door to ask for a night's lodging. Most times, the traveler was a scientist, either a geologist with a box of stones, or an astronomer in quest of a dark night. Sometimes it was a poet. Other times simply an adventurer looking for spots yet undiscovered and far from the beaten path.

So rare were such visits that each one seemed like a big event. The Poloverdo woman would pour a drink from a chipped pitcher with shaky hands. The Poloverdo man would force himself to say two words to the stranger so as not to seem too boorish. But he was still a boor, and his wife unfailingly poured the wine outside the glass. All the while the wind would hiss through the disjointed window, sounding like the howling of wolves.

When the visitor departed, the man and the woman would close their door with a sigh of relief. Their solitude resumed its course on the desolate moor, among the rocks and the violent elements.

The Poloverdos had a child. A boy, who was born out of their bedroom routine, without particular love, and who grew like all the rest on this land, that is to say not very well. He spent his days hunting for snakes. He had dirt under his nails, his ears had been so beaten down by storms that they looked like flaps, his skin was yellow and dry, and his teeth were as white as pieces of salt. His name was Paolo. Paolo Poloverdo.

Paolo was the one who saw the man arrive on the path, one warm January day. And he was the one who ran to warn his parents that a stranger was coming. Except that this time, it was not a geologist, or an adventurer, and even less a poet. It was Angel Allegria. A vagrant, a crook, a murderer. And he was not arriving by chance at this house at the end of the world. The Poloverdo woman took her pitcher. Her eyes met those of Angel Allegria—small eyes, deeply set, as if pushed into their sockets by blows; eyes that betrayed a brutal wickedness. She shook more than usual. Her man sat on the bench facing the vagrant.

"Will you stay here long?" he asked.

"Yes," answered the other. He dipped his lips in the wine. Outside, rain clouds were coming up from the sea. Paolo had gone out of the house. He was waiting for the first drops to fall, his face turned to the sky and his mouth open. Like all the creatures on this land, he was always thirsty. The poets who had come to visit had compared him to a seed planted in the bedrock, condemned never to bloom.

While the first drops came crashing down onto the dust and onto Paolo's tongue, Angel Allegria took out his knife and planted it in the man's throat, then in the woman's. On the table, the wine and the blood mingled, forever reddening the deep grooves of the wood.

This was not Angel's first crime. Death was commonplace where he came from. It put an end to debts, drunken disputes, women's deceptions, neighbors' betrayals, or simply ended the monotony of a dull day. This time it put an end to two weeks of wandering. Angel was tired of sleeping outdoors, of fleeing south a little more each morning. He had heard that this house was the last one before the desert and the sea, the ideal refuge for a hunted man. It was here that he wanted to sleep.

When Paolo came back, soaked to the bones, he discovered his parents lying on the ground, and he understood. Angel was waiting for him, knife in hand.

"Come here," Angel told him.

Paolo did not move. He stared at the sullied blade, at the hand holding the knife, at the arm that did not shake. The rain drummed on the metallic roof, as if announcing a trapeze artist's somersault at the circus.

"How old are you?" Angel asked.

"I don't know," Paolo answered.

"Can you make soup?"

Angel had a firm grip on the handle of his knife, and yet remained undecided. The child, very small, very dirty, very wet, stood in front of him, and he could not imagine putting an end to his life. An unexpected twist of his conscience, maybe a little pity, held back his arm.

"I've never killed a child," he said.

"Neither have I," said Paolo.

The answer made Angel smile.

"Can you make soup, or not?" he asked again.

"I think so."

"Make me some soup, then."

Angel put his knife away. He was sparing the child, and with some relief told himself that he did not need to kill him. The little one would not prevent him from sleeping here; besides, it would be convenient to send the boy to fetch water at the well rather than go himself.

Paolo headed for the back of the house, entered a dark recess where his mother kept some meager supplies, and soon came out with a few potatoes, a leek, a turnip, and a piece of dried-up lard. He knew how to make soup, although he had never made any. He had watched his mother so often that the recipe was imprinted in his mind. To make a fire, he only had to imitate his father's gestures. It was easy.

Once the soup was ready, he turned to Angel Allegria.

"Serve me," said the killer.

Paolo went to fetch one of his father's iron bowls, the largest one, and put it on the table, far from the blood and wine stain. He poured the soup into it.

"Eat with me," Angel ordered.

Paolo went to fetch another bowl, the smallest and most dented one, his own. He helped himself and sat on the bench, facing the man, who was already slurping his soup. The rain had stopped. It was not cold in the house, thanks to the fire that crackled in the fireplace. Behind the window, night was coming like an ocean wave about to engulf the house and drown the world. Paolo lit a candle.

"Come on, eat," Angel told him.

The soup smelled good. But the eyes of the child wandered and stared at the lifeless bodies stretched on the ground. He put his hands around the bowl but was unable to bring it to his mouth. The killer turned and looked at the two corpses.

"Is that why you've lost your appetite?" he asked.

Paolo nodded. Angel Allegria got up from his bench, sighing.

"Well then." He went to rummage in the recess and found a shovel. "Come," he said, "I need you to hold the light."

Paolo took the storm lantern, lit it, and went into the

night with the man. He saw him pull his parents' bodies along the rocks.

"The soil is hard," Paolo warned.

Worse than hard. It took Angel two hours to dig a hole hardly large enough for the man and woman. The shovel knocked against the stones and the roots. The handle burned his hands. Finally, he succeeded in putting the corpses in the hole; he covered it, packed the ground on the knoll, and, out of habit, wiped his forehead. Yet the wind coming from the sea had dried his skin: he had hardly perspired.

"Are you happy now?" he asked the child, roughly.

Paolo held the lamp up to his face and looked at the grave. For a brief moment he wanted to bury himself in the ground, to sleep, but he knew that he did not have the right to do so, since he was not dead. He understood that on this desolate land, only the dead were entitled to peace. The others, the living, had no choice but to clench their teeth and endure life. This was the gift that Angel had just given to Paolo: a life. But what kind of life?

"Come," the man said. "There is nothing more to see, and the soup will be cold."

CHAPTER TWO

ANGEL ALLEGRIA WAS a wanted man. The police of Talcahuano, Temuco, and Puerto Natales were looking for him. In these three cities, he had robbed old ladies, swindled young people, and killed those who resisted him. His victims had no face, and he himself never had occasion to look in a mirror. His world seethed with silhouettes, with threatening shadows that he brushed aside as if chasing away swarms of flies.

When young, he had seen his father die. As for his mother, he had hardly known her. Early on, he had learned to fend for himself, following the harsh rules of the streets to survive.

The only things he had ever possessed were his knife, his physical strength, and the stolen money that quickly slipped through his fingers. Once or twice he thought he was in love with a woman but none had been able to soften his fiery temper. These affairs had ended like everything else, in bitterness, in shouts of accusations, and in angry stomps down fire escapes. Angel Allegria was not a respectable person, especially not one fit to bring up a child.

Nevertheless, here he was living with Paolo, in this house cornered by the winds, the rains, the snows, and the skies. Paolo, young and ignorant, did not have a choice. The murderer had installed himself in his house and he had to put up with him.

Both of them tended to the vegetable garden, to the chickens and the goats. Paolo kept making soup and hunting for snakes, although less than before because Angel did not like him to search between the stones. "You're going to get bitten," he would say, "and you will be sorry."

What really puzzled Angel was the age of the child. Paolo's small body wasn't a reliable indicator. He appeared to be five, but could as well have been eight or ten years old.

"Try to remember when you were born," Angel would say.

"I was born the day you arrived," the child would answer.

"Not at all!"

"I don't remember anything before that day."

What was Angel supposed to think? Had he, through

the hazard of circumstance, become the child's father? After all, why not? He was almost thirty-five years old and, so far, had never done anything good in his life. To be a father, well, that was something meaningful.

"Call me Papa," he said one day.

"No."

"It's an order."

Paolo shook his head. "My father lies here, under this," he answered, showing the mound.

Angel turned away. The grave, which lay in the middle of the path leading to the vegetable garden, had begun to torment him. Its silent presence was a constant reminder of his past misdeeds. It was proof of his cruelty, stupid actions, and helplessness. Paolo put wildflowers there sometimes. His eyes remained dry but they tried to probe through the depth of the soil like the drills of an oil digger. All the questions that the child did not ask, and all the answers also, were buried there. Angel always felt a little jealous to see him stop in front of the mound.

"We could flatten it," he said.

"Why?"

"To open the path."

"The path is large enough."

Angel looked around him. It was true. How could this pile of dirt be in the way, considering the vast and desertlike stretch of land surrounding it? He did not dare talk about it again. It was agreed: the grave would remain as it was.

"But you and I, we could leave," Angel suggested.

"Go if you want," said Paolo. "Me, I live here."

"I live here too. And anyway, I can't leave. I'd be arrested by the police."

A full year went by and no one came to the Poloverdo house. You would have believed that word had spread among the geologists, the adventurers, and the stargazers to avoid the place; that they knew what a brutal owner they would find there. So solitude closed its arms around the desolate house, cradling it with its empty voice to lull it to sleep.

When the rain damaged the metallic roof, Angel climbed to repair it.

When the snow covered the vegetable garden, Angel held Paolo close to him at night to keep warm.

When the winds howled under the window and door, Angel repaired them to keep the draft out.

He wondered why, in the past, he had ever felt the need to steal, kill, and cheat, when it seemed so easy to live without bothering anyone, simply fighting the seasons and the roughness of life, with the presence of the child as his only joy.

"In town, people live on top of each other," he said to Paolo. "That's why they're so nervous."

"Is it why you became a killer?" the child asked.

"I don't know."

"Why didn't you kill me?"

"Maybe you didn't make me nervous."

Then, as the summer began to whiten the metallic roof and the snakes hid in the shade of the rocks, a traveler was seen approaching the house. Angel was coming back from the well, carrying plastic containers that made his arms ache. The man signaled to him. Angel glanced toward the garden where the child was hoeing, waiting for the water. He felt a pain in his stomach. The old mistrust was creeping back. From the distance, the man seemed young and strong, and probably was, since you had to be in good health to walk up to this spot. Who was he?

"Hello!" said the stranger. "I'm looking for the Poloverdo farm. Is this it?"

Angel went on the path, the containers banging against his thighs. Already, the fear of danger made the hair on his arms stand on end. Over in the garden, Paolo had stopped hoeing: he had heard the man call.

"You are Mr. Poloverdo?" the stranger asked.

"What do you want?" Angel put the containers down in front of the stranger's feet.

Although they were stained with mud and dust, Angel could see that the man's walking shoes were new. The quality of his clothing indicated that he was rich. He was tall, well built, jovial and sure of himself. Anyone but Angel would have found him pleasant.

"My name is Luis Secunda," the man said, holding out his hand.

Angel did not bother to shake it. He folded his arms

across his chest. If he had to kill this man, he preferred to avoid any preliminary contact. In the meantime, Paolo had joined them and the stranger smiled at him broadly.

"I realize that I am disturbing you. . . ."

"That's right," said Angel.

"It's okay," said Paolo. "Would you like a drink?"

The child made the offer spontaneously, without thinking. He went to open the door to the house.

"Come in," he said.

"Hurry!" Angel grumbled. "Don't let the heat in."

They quickly entered the darkness of the small house. Angel kicked a chicken that ran off cackling.

"You're not badly off here," the stranger remarked. "You're right to live away from everything. The city . . ."

Out of habit, the child had taken out his mother's chipped pitcher to pour a glass of goat's milk for his guest.

". . . the city is hell," the stranger went on.

He drank the goat's milk in one gulp. Angel sat down on the bench facing him and watched him surreptitiously. His knife was in the drawer, within easy reach. Under the stranger's elbows, in the grooves of the table, traces of Paolo's parents' blood still remained. Now the stranger had a white mustache above his lip from the cream of the milk. Inwardly, Angel was fuming at Paolo: a glass of milk! He knew how precious it was here!

"I'm looking for a special place," the stranger explained. "A place . . . how can I put it? . . . a place like this one."

"You mean like this house?" Paolo asked, surprised.

"Like this house. Like this path. Like the rocks." The stranger got up and went to the window. "Like this sky and those low bushes, over there. A place exactly like this one."

He turned to look at the man and the child; he was smiling.

"Like this place, hmmm . . . ," Angel muttered. "But not *this* one."

The stranger came back and sat down again. The more Angel looked at him, the more he was sure of the inevitable end: he was going to kill this man. By disturbing their peace, the intruder had sealed his fate and put an end to the truce. The hellish cycle was about to start again; already Angel felt a tingling in his fingers.

"I know that I am intruding," Luis Secunda continued awkwardly, "but—"

"Would you like some more milk?" Paolo interrupted.

He poured another glass of milk while Angel continued to fume, his fists clenched under the table. The drawer was not far. It wouldn't take much effort.

"I'm willing to pay you," the stranger went on. "Money is not a problem for me. I have more than I need. And I'm willing to work. If you agreed, I could rent out part of your land and build a shack. I don't want to take advantage of your hospitality. I would go to the far end of the path, where you would hardly see me."

Paolo had put the empty pitcher down on the table and was looking at Angel. He sensed that a tragedy was about to happen if he did not intervene. He liked the stranger. He did not want him to die. He also did not feel like helping Angel dig a new hole. The drought of these last weeks had made the soil more compact and denser than granite. It was difficult enough to dig the furrows in the garden. When he saw that Angel was opening the drawer, he cried out:

"Oh, Papa! That would be so nice, Papa! Say yes, Papa!"

Angel froze. *Papa.* Had the child really said "Papa"?

"Your son is a nice kid," the stranger said. "I'm sure he's been well brought up."

Angel remained stunned, his hand suspended above the drawer.

"Come on, Papa," implored Paolo. "Please, Papa."

CHAPTER THREE

WHEN HE WAS thirty years old, Luis Secunda had left Valparaiso to travel around the world. In his family, it was unheard of to remain in the place where you were born. Of Spanish origin, generations of Secundas had scattered throughout the seven continents. Luis's mother got stranded in Valparaiso after many years of senseless journeys. There, she finished the education of her four children—all miraculously fathered by the same man—before leaving for Africa to follow a new lover.

Luis's father, a rich wine merchant, lavishly provided his children with money, thinking that this kind of fertilizer would ensure their blossoming. He sent checks the way others send postcards. Each time he came back to Valparaiso from his travels, he inspected his four offspring with the same care he brought to his vines. Satisfied that they were growing in size, and unable to measure anything else, he would leave again, his conscience at peace.

Luis's two older sisters married young, one a German, the other a Frenchman, and both had left Chile. His younger brother had dreams that took him to Hollywood, where he hoped to become an actor. When his father had last visited Valparaiso, Luis was the only one still living in the family house.

"You're still here?" Mr. Secunda had said, surprised.

"I guess I'm the kind that puts down roots," Luis answered.

"Well, put down roots where you want, but not here. I'm selling the house."

These last years, the wine business had not been particularly good. Expenses needed to be cut, and belt-tightening often meant that one had to sell.

"Here is your share," Luis's father told him. "This is the last time I'll give you money. And this is my last visit to Valparaiso. From now on, you'll have to fend for yourself."

It was then that Luis left the city of his birth, imagining that he would travel around the world. After all, it was the most natural thing for a Secunda to do, even if it was the most unlikely thing for Luis.

When he said goodbye to his friends and girlfriends, he made the solemn promise to write to them from the farthest and most exotic cities. He saw the excitement in their eyes: *Luis Secunda is going around the world! He is a fantastic man!* they must have been thinking.

"And then?" Paolo asked when Luis told him his story.

"Then, nothing. I took a train going south. I slept in hotels. I walked the streets. . . ."

"Did you like it?"

"No."

"So, you didn't even leave Chile?"

"I arrived here."

"And the letters?"

"Promises are not always kept, you know."

Paolo nodded with seriousness. He grasped only half of what Luis meant, since no one had ever promised him anything. What he did understand was that Luis was trying to escape from something, a little as an ostrich would. He had found this no-man's-land, and it was here that he was hiding his shame. In Valparaiso, he'd left the impression that he was a fearless adventurer, and now he was condemned to keep the dream alive for his friends by disappearing.

"What do you see in this stranger?" Angel asked with annoyance when Paolo came back from the shack at the end of the path.

"Nothing. I'm just helping him build his roof."

"Let him cope by himself. Come and help me look after the goat instead."

Paolo followed Angel to the goats' enclosure. There were five of them, no longer young, that Paolo's father had bought at a fair a long time before. They were still giving milk, but not much. One of them had been ill for a few weeks.

"You know, I don't think it's sick," Paolo grumbled as he sat astride the fence.

Angel was already near the goat, which was bleating weakly, and forced it to lie down. He brandished a vial filled with a vitamin solution.

"Of course it's sick! It's dragging itself. It's in pain and its eyes are lifeless!"

Paolo let Angel take care of the goat. Vitamins wouldn't hurt it, but there was no miracle cure for old age. Looking at Angel, at this murderer, who was trying everything possible to save the life of an old goat, made Paolo feel he was caught in a whirlwind. How were such actions possible? How could anyone comprehend the universe without first understanding the ways of the people they lived with?

"I'm going snake hunting," he said suddenly.

In spite of Angel's protests, he ran off, far from the house, far from the goats' enclosure, far from the mound where his parents' bodies were rotting, and far from Luis's rickety shack. He ran like a frightened rabbit. This immense space, relentlessly assaulted by the wind and pounded by the sun—this infinite space—was his, deeper and darker than an abyss. Since his younger years he had known that the cold waters of the Pacific lay beyond this flat and barren land where he lived. He could also just make out the distant shapes of volcanoes. The tales told by the travelers had sown seeds in his mind, where they had flowered into words unknown to him before. Words like *city, fair, ship, observatory, Temuco, Valparaiso, train, horses, storms* . . .

He stopped running. Around him, the rocks resembled an impassive and dead forest. He did not feel like chasing snakes. He sat on the ground and watched the clouds march from the sea like an army ready to invade and darken the land.

❖

After sunset, Angel started to get anxious. He had waited. Now he was worried about Paolo. And he was upset with himself for worrying. Only apprehensive mothers worried, not murderers. He searched for Paolo by going round the outside of the house, the storm lantern in hand. Then he went to the vegetable garden, came back toward the mound, which he passed with sorrow, and went down the path. At the end of the path, he made out the light that the stranger had attached to the ceiling of his shack. It was swaying in the night, irritating him. Angel's fists tightened: if he found Paolo at the stranger's house, he determined he would go back home to fetch his knife. And this time, "Papa" or not, he would kill him for having stolen the affection of the child.

He reached the shack, very angry at Luis. A hinge broke as soon as he gave the first blow on the door. The stranger was startled when he saw Angel. He was alone.

"What can I do for you?" he asked.

"Paolo is not here?"

"No."

Angel showed him the hinge. "You work like a pig. This doesn't even hold."

"I'll fix it."

Luis took a closer look at Angel's distressed face.

"I can look for him with you, if you like. Together we'll be more efficient."

Angel shrugged. This man, with his educated way of speaking, and his stupid uncalled-for smiles, annoyed him. But he was right. To look for the child, two people would be better than one. Once Paolo was found, he swore to himself that he would get his knife and rid himself of Luis once and for all.

A strong wind was sweeping the ground, raising dust that stung the skin, eyes, and throat. Clouds were unraveling against the starry sky, letting a large pinkish moon appear at times.

Equipped with lanterns, the two men set out into the wild darkness. Their hearts were pounding madly, their eyes darted like those of wary deer, and their throats became hoarse from shouting.

"Paolo-o-o-o! Paolo-o-o-o!"

After searching for fifteen minutes, Luis stopped and pulled on Angel's sleeve.

"Let's split up. I'll go west; you keep going east."

Angel put his hand firmly on Luis. What kind of trick was this? He thought he knew what was in the eyes of the stranger: *he* wanted to find Paolo and brag about it, making himself even more likable to the child.

"You keep going east!" Angel shouted. "*I'm* going west."

"As you wish . . ."

Luis went off, pushed by the winds, protecting the light with his free hand. Angel tried hard to understand. He wished he were shrewder and better educated so as to be sure that this man was not going to trick him. He felt as if his small brain were locking thoughts inside, smothering and compressing them, and that his skull would never be large enough to let intelligence bloom. This thought cramped his face with pain.

"Paolo-o-o-o!" he heard Luis shout.

Angel shook himself and turned west, his face whipped by the wind. Intelligent or not, he was determined to find the child. Then he would kill the stranger, and everything would be calm again. He started to walk, mad with rage, his lamp held as high as a lighthouse in the middle of the sea.

"Paolo-o-o-o!"

He hit a rock and his leg started to bleed under his pants. The pain took his breath away. The wind was howling in his ears. The dust blinded him and dried his tears.

He resumed his walk, carefully sidestepping the rocks, which seemed to have grown like trees. And suddenly, as he extended his hand to avoid hurting himself again, another hand gripped his own.

"Angel, is that you?" Paolo said in a quavering voice.

"Yes, I'm here."

"You found me?"

"Yes."

Paolo's small hand was icy. He had probably fallen asleep, only to have the nighttime take him by surprise.

Angel gripped the lantern ring with his teeth and, without effort, lifted the child in his arms. He opened his vest, wrapped Paolo in it close to his warm body, then headed back to the house. The pain was gone. He felt only huge relief and pride to have found the child alive. This feeling radiated so strongly inside him that he decided to delay the murder of the stranger and enjoy this extraordinary moment. A moment when he was walking, a body nestled against his, with the certainty that he was accomplishing something important in the world.

CHAPTER FOUR

THE OLD GOAT died in spite of the vitamins and tender care.

Angel never showed how upset he was and forced himself to carve up the animal. He would have liked to bury it close to the mound where Paolo's parents were resting, but meat was too scarce to allow for sentimentality. He cooked the best pieces and made a rather good pâté that he gave to Paolo, who, in turn, offered some to Luis. That was the way it was now, and Angel had to accept sharing the pâté, the goat's milk, and the love of the child. In return, Luis always made sure to fill the water tank and to grow a few potatoes, as well as tend to a plant from whose large leaves he made a grayish tobacco that now and again he brought to Angel in a small silver-clasped box. The two men would smoke together on the doorstep of the house as they watched the last rays of the sun die on the horizon. Peace, at least a kind of peace, had grown between them. Angel's knife remained in the drawer, next to the corkscrew and the nutcracker.

⁜

With the first autumnal wind, the roof of the shack was blown away and Luis had no choice but to seek refuge in the house.

"Come in," Paolo said, opening the door wide.

"Hurry up!" Angel grumbled. "Don't let the dampness in."

Luis entered and sat on the bench, across from where Angel was plucking a chicken. On the table he put a leather bag that contained the precious things he wanted to save.

"Push that away," Angel said. "Can't you see the feathers and the blood everywhere?"

The headless chicken was losing blood. Its feathers were flying about the room and reddened as they landed in the puddles of blood. Paolo was busy with the fire, restocking the twigs that were constantly falling. At the end of summer, he had gone with Angel on an exhausting trip to the edge of the desolate stretch of land, right where the forest began. They had brought back the young firewood, which was now smoking in the fireplace.

Luis sat near the blaze with his bag on his knees and sadly gazed at the flames. Angel glanced at him, fearful that Luis would launch into one of his speeches, which always fascinated Paolo.

"What's in your bag?" the child asked.

Angel grabbed a clump of feathers in one of his large murderous hands and pulled on it briskly.

Luis sighed. "Papers, a book—"

"A book?" Paolo said, surprised.

Paolo had seen books once or twice before, when poets or scientists had visited. One of them had even tried to teach him to read, but Paolo did not remember the lesson.

"Do you want to see it?" asked Luis.

"He doesn't have time," Angel said. He moved toward the fireplace, holding the plucked chicken as if it were a cudgel. "Here! The chicken is ready for roasting."

Paolo caught the chicken on the fly and smiled.

"I can cook the chicken and listen to the book at the same time," he pointed out.

Angel had no answer. The child was beginning to think like a city person; that was what came of socializing with the stranger! This man was definitely a bad influence, and Angel regretted not having killed him the very day he had showed up. It was too late now. Paolo had grown attached to Luis. Angel knew that he would lose the confidence of the child if he were to kill the man now. Just like meat, the child's confidence was precious to him: in fact, Angel had discovered that it was far more nourishing than any pâté. Who else had trusted him these past thirty-five years? No one. He had never before felt a human being cling to him without reservation, as he had on the unforgettable night that he had saved the child from the darkness and the biting cold.

Luis opened his bag. He took the book out. It was old, its pages turned yellow; his wine merchant father had given it to him, together with a purse filled with gold coins. The gift had surprised Luis. Even more so since the book was a collection of poetry.

"Did your father love poems?" Paolo asked.

"No. But poets like wine. One of them bought a bottle with this book. My father never opened it."

As the chicken roasted on the spit and filled the house with a savory aroma, Luis began to read. Angel stationed himself in front of the window, hands deep in his pockets, as he listened to the crackling of the words, the fire, and the chicken fat dripping onto the wood. The poem spoke of ancient mariners who were thrown back to shore like seaweed, and who looked gaunt after witnessing so many men perish in the storms. It spoke of nature and feelings of the heart with simplicity and courage. As he listened and watched the rain batter against the window, Angel was soothed by the words and surprised that he understood them easily. These words were finding a way into his narrow mind; it was as if the rain were nourishing his body while clearing away the grit and clods of dirt.

From that day on, the two men and the child lived together in the house. Each night, Luis opened the book and read aloud while the soup steamed. Each night, Angel stood in front of the window so that the others would not notice his tears, the tears that wetted his killer's eyes.

CHAPTER FIVE

IN HIS BAG, Luis also had some paper and some pens. The white sheets of paper were arranged neatly in a folder, and the pens were of various colors. These material things made it possible to express the immaterial, and both paper and pens patiently waited to be used by Luis in his travels around the world.

"Why don't you try?" Paolo asked as he stroked the paper with the back of his hand.

"To go around the world, you mean?" said Luis. "I don't have the will to. You see, I'm like the vine that can grow only in a certain type of soil, on the slopes of such and such a hillside, and has to be exposed to a certain angle of the sun's rays. If you move me, I die."

Paolo thought Luis was exaggerating. He had come from Valparaiso to this place and he had not died. For Paolo, who had never boarded a train, or a boat, Valparaiso was as far away as Madrid or the Marquesas Islands.

"In faraway countries," Luis said, trying to convince him, "people speak foreign languages that I don't understand. They eat strange-looking and weird-tasting vegetables; the water they drink would make me sick; the climate would make me perspire and give me headaches. Travel can bring lots of inconveniences and unpleasant surprises."

"Here, too, there are unpleasant surprises," Paolo objected. "The goat died, and then the roof of your shack blew away."

"My roof was very fragile, and the goat was old," Luis answered.

Paolo was about to mention his parents, whose lives had also been taken away, but he changed his mind. What good would it do to talk about them now? He could hardly remember the sounds of their voices, or their smell; and besides, Angel wouldn't want him to linger on the past. Only the present was important.

It was raining outside. Angel had gone out, wearing a waterproof poncho that had belonged to Paolo's father. He had announced that he was going for some "fresh air."

Luis was watching the cloudbursts knock on the window

and wondered how Angel could stay out so long under this deluge. He couldn't have guessed that it would have been more painful for Angel to watch him teach the child how to write; that this deluge of knowledge would have been worse than the cloudbursts coming down from the skies. As soon as he had seen the sheets of paper and the pens, he had fetched the poncho.

"And what if you wrote, anyway?" Paolo asked Luis.

Luis saw the child's shining eyes. They were like two gleaming chestnuts freshly out of their burrs. Paolo had never seen anyone write. His illiterate parents had been unable to hold a pen, and Angel was not much better.

"Let's write together," Luis suggested. "A word each."

Words were like snakes. They slipped between Paolo's fingers, escaped and teased him. He thought he could catch one, but the smooth curves of the letters required so much skill that after a fifteen-minute chase, Paolo's sheet of paper was covered with strange signs, erasures, and blotches.

"It's difficult," he said.

"True," Luis muttered. "It requires a lot of effort at the beginning."

He was thinking that he would not send any letters as long as Paolo was unable to write, and so his friends would not know of his cowardice. The ignorance of the child would protect him a while longer; but a time would come when it would not be possible to escape. He put the pens away.

"Don't you want to teach me anymore?" Paolo asked.

"Of course I do, but you have to go slowly."

Paolo was hesitant in his desire. He guessed that his power would be great once he mastered the snake-words. At the same time, he knew he would lose something precious. It would be the same as when he had gained Angel's friendship and protection: in exchange he had lost his parents. Nothing, he understood, came free.

Luis put the sheets of paper back in his bag. Just then, Angel opened the door. He walked in, his poncho dripping, and soon steam rose up around him as it did from the tops of the volcanoes that one could see far in the west. From the folds of the poncho, he took out a ball of wet fur, which he displayed in the dying light of the fire. He had just found a lost fox cub. The animal had a head wound and some damage on one of its legs, but it was alive. Angel had walked far from the house, toward the trees of the forest, where he had heard plaintive cries through the whistling of the winds and the drumming of the rain on his cap.

He came near Paolo, whose eyes were wide open with wonder.

"It's for you," said Angel. "Do whatever you want with it."

Paolo took the cub in his arms. A delicate fur covered the animal's head. The fox was so light that Paolo suddenly felt as strong as a giant. As he carried the wounded fox against his chest, he felt a much greater strength than if he had been able to write all the words in the world. He looked at Angel gratefully and crouched in front of the hearth to warm the cub.

Angel got rid of his poncho. He hung it on a hook, and soon the dripping rain formed a puddle on the floor.

"Is it really safe to keep this animal?" Luis inquired.

Angel glanced at him with a challenging look. The city dweller might be good at showing off with his books and his pens, but he would never be able to rival nature's vitality, beauty, and wildness.

"It could bite," Luis objected.

"No, no, I will tame him," Paolo said.

Angel smiled and sat on the bench, the silver-clasped box on his knees. Enough tobacco remained for two cigarettes. He rolled them slowly, then offered one to Luis.

In front of the fire, Paolo had curled up with the cub in the fold of his belly. Before falling asleep, he muttered: "It will need milk since it's a baby, won't it, Angel?"

That night, Luis did not read. That night, Angel had won.

CHAPTER SIX

THE FALL WENT by, then the winter. The task of daily chores—cooking, keeping the fire going, repairing the damage caused by the harshness of the seasons, caring for the goats, collecting the eggs of the chickens . . . even sleeping while listening to the roar of the storms—kept everyone busy. Luis was torn between his desire to help Paolo grow up and the cowardice that constantly pushed him to delay. So the book of poems gathered a fine coat of dust during the harsh winter months. Besides, it was so cold on some evenings that Luis's numbed fingers would have been unable to turn the pages.

Thanks to Paolo's tender care and to the goat's milk, the

fox cub healed and reached its adult size long before Paolo could even draw the letters of his name with a steady hand. When the first sunny days of spring arrived, and the temperature began to jump above the freezing point, the cub's appetite increased. It needed meat.

Paolo started hunting, determined to be the only provider for his pet. He armed himself with an ice pick from the shed and went out every morning to look for moles or voles; anything as long as it could please his fox.

Only snakes were to be found on the desolate land. Therefore Paolo had to venture far from the house, in the direction of the trees. He never entered the forest. This dark and vertical universe frightened him. His search stopped on the outskirts of the forest, and when a small appetizing animal appeared, he would hurry to corner it before the creature had the idea of fleeing into the woods. This fear of the dense vegetation hampered Paolo, and he often came back with an empty bag.

In the house, the fox began to yelp and growl. Paolo had to attach it to a stake, but the animal would twist its leash until it almost strangled itself. Luis avoided passing within its reach. As for Angel, he observed the fox, fascinated by its pointed teeth, and eagerly waited for the day when the animal would no longer contain its violent tendencies. He was certain that since he was tall and strong, the animal would attack Luis rather than him or Paolo, who was his master and friend. Angel no longer wished to get rid of Luis, but he had a constant need to belittle him, to show him who had the upper hand.

"You're afraid of the fox, aren't you?" he asked mockingly.

"Yes," Luis confessed.

"It's your fear that makes it nervous."

"No, it's hunger. What about giving it one of our chickens?"

"*Our* chickens?"

"All right . . . one of *your* chickens."

"Absolutely not."

❖

When the weather improved, Luis went for long walks, far from the fox and far from Angel, whom he considered mad and not much better than an animal. He would walk for hours until his feet were worn out.

One day he reached the sea inlet very, very far to the west. Surprised by this discovery, Luis contemplated the icy waters and the pieces of iceberg that drifted along. The weather was so clear that he could make out the snow-covered tops of the volcanoes in the distance. Confronted as he was by so much beauty, his loneliness and confusion gave rise to bits of phrases and words that exploded in his mind like fireworks. He felt sorry he had not taken his bag along.

Later on, he walked back to the house and found an

even more surprising sight: the table was overturned and so was the bench, the ashes of the fireplace were spread all over the room, and, in an awful silence, Angel and Paolo stood facing the fox. The animal was crouched in the recess leading to the nook, and it was growling and showing its fangs. It had broken from its leash. Its ears down, eyes shining, it seemed about to leap.

"Don't move!" Angel ordered.

Luis remained frozen in the open doorway.

Next to Angel, Paolo was crying silently, his body shaking. He was holding the ice pick, pointing it timidly at the fox.

Angel took a step toward the table. The fox went back on its haunches a little more. Angel took another step. The fox growled ferociously.

"Come closer to me," Angel told Paolo softly. "Slowly, like that . . ."

Paolo was sniffling, and his mouth was distorted by fear and pain. When he came elbow to elbow with Angel, he tried talking to the animal.

"Relax, nobody wants to hurt you. I am your friend. You and me, you know that. I promise that tomorrow you'll have enough to eat. I'll bring you a whole doe and—"

The fox growled louder, curling its chops.

"And what if this beast has rabies?" Luis whispered.

Gusts of wind were rushing into the house, blowing the ashes around, while the ceiling lamp swung on the hook. Angel took another step forward. He was only a few inches from the overturned table. He moved his arm very slowly toward the drawer. The knife was there, within his reach. He opened the drawer very gently, his eyes never leaving the beast. Suddenly, the fox sprang. One would have thought that it had been catapulted by an invisible and powerful machine. Its leap was so precise, so swift, that Angel hardly had time to cover his face with his arms. The fox swooped down on him, its muzzle wide open. Angel screamed.

"No-o-o!" shouted Paolo.

Luis stood still. The cold was biting his back. He had the feeling he had become an iceberg, one of the inert blocks of ice he had seen earlier, armless, legless, unable to help the man who was crying out in pain.

"Paolo!" Angel shouted. "Kill it! Kill it!"

Luis turned to the child. Paolo was looking at the tip of the ice pick in his hands, then at the fox, then at Angel, then again at the ice pick. In spite of his size and strength, Angel was unable to shake off the fox. They were both rolling on the ash-covered ground as though pushed around by the wind. The jaw of the fox was clenched on Angel's shoulder.

"Kill it! Kill it!"

Paolo gave a start. One last time, he looked at the tip of the ice pick. At the fox. Then he threw himself forward. Luis closed his eyes. All he heard were screams, yelps, cries, and panting. When he finally dared to look, he saw a shape-less heap: the man, the child, the fox—all three were entangled together, stained with blood, sweat, and tears.

Angel was the first to emerge from the pack, his shoulder, his cheek, his left ear bleeding. He knelt down in front of the child and pulled him away. Paolo's face was filled with distress and he was still holding the ice pick with both hands. The tip had broken off, half of it embedded in the flesh and fur of the fox.

"Paolo," Angel said softly.

"I killed it?"

"Yes."

"Is that what you wanted?"

"Yes."

The child let go of the ice pick. His body went limp.

Luis saw Paolo's torn heart reflected on the child's face and realized that with this incident Paolo had left his childhood behind. He also realized that this was going to affect his own life and that of Angel's just as brutally.

At the end of the rocky path, in this house battered by the southern winds, there were now three lonely men, and a fox to bury.

CHAPTER SEVEN

JANUARY WAS HERE again. Luis's tobacco plants were blooming, the dirt of the vegetable garden was cracking like old varnish, the potatoes were easily confused for stones, two more goats were showing signs of old age, and Paolo's eyes were no longer shining like fresh chestnuts. Angel's shoulder was healing. There was a small bulge next to the mound of dirt.

Angel and Luis spent many early evenings on the doorstep, smoking in the sunset. The air was heavy. To distract Paolo from his sadness, Luis pushed him to resume his lessons. He already could write several words: *Paolo—Angel—Luis—Chile—fox—knife*.

"Do you want to learn a new word?" Luis asked one night while opening his bag.

"I don't know."

"There are a lot of words, but only a few letters to spell them. It won't be difficult to learn them all."

Angel slid along the bench to come closer to them. He had let his guard down. He no longer feared the sheets of paper and the pens. All he wanted was to see a smile on Paolo's face, whatever the price to pay.

"Come on, Paolo, show me how you do it," he said encouragingly.

"Are you really interested?"

"Of course I am."

Suspicious, Paolo took a black pen. *Angel—Chile— fox—knife*, he wrote. Strands of his long straight hair fell on the paper and made a grating noise under the pen. He jerked his head to push them back. Angel observed his face. The child's features had hardened but were not yet showing any signs of puberty. How old could this boy be? Angel regretted having killed the Poloverdo woman without asking her first.

"In your opinion, Luis, how old is Paolo?"

The writing lesson finished, Paolo had gone off, leaving the two men alone.

"I would say ten or eleven years old," Luis said. "Is that right?"

"I don't know."

"You're his father and you don't know? How can that be?"

Angel remembered that he had kept the lie alive from the first day, when Paolo had prevented him from committing another crime by calling him Papa.

"Fathers are not like mothers," he said simply.

Luis pulled a chair outside and sat facing the sky. He remembered his own father, who knew precisely what were the good years for wines, but always forgot the birth dates of his children. He understood what Angel meant.

"And his mother, where is she?"

"Dead."

Luis watched Paolo, who was weeding the garden farther down. His eyes went to the mound of dirt.

"That's sad," he said.

"Yes."

Surprisingly, Angel really was feeling sad. As he sat surrounded by the melancholic and sweeping light, in this empty and disconsolate place, time was passing by, senseless, endless, and he could see the day coming when he would lose Paolo's affection. Without the child's love, he would again become what he actually was, a murderer, a thief, a crook, a parasite whose life was of no importance to anyone.

He threw his cigarette on the ground and crushed it with his foot. His mouth was on fire; he was thirsty. He went back inside the house and reached for the pitcher. It slipped from his hands. He saw it fall at his feet and break into a thousand pieces.

Luis put his head inside the door. "What happened?" he asked.

Angel remained stunned. The chunks of clay, the shards at his feet, they were the broken pieces of his heart. His throat tightened. He fell on his knees and yet did not have the strength to gather the mess. Sobs were shaking his whole body.

Luis came and crouched by his side. Without understanding the reason for Angel's tears, he felt a great compassion. This brute, this uneducated, dour man was crying! He put his hand on Angel's arm. There were so many reasons to cry, after all! The broken pitcher, the cold, the hunger, the solitude, the banishment, the shipwrecks, the mothers who left one day to follow their lovers, the fathers who thought that giving gold coins was a way to please, the nights spent contemplating the sea in Valparaiso, the absence of women, the unattainable dreams, the marvelous poems one has forgotten, the betrayed children, the dead foxes, the fear of living, all these reasons and many more were enough to make anyone sad.

The two men were kneeling on the floor when Paolo found them. He had come back from the garden, his forehead shining with sweat. He wanted to drink some water from the pitcher. He squinted, uncertain of what he was seeing. When Luis and Angel turned toward him with red eyes and wet cheeks, Paolo knew he was not dreaming.

That very night, he added a new word to the list of those he already could write: *pitcher.*

A few days later, two of the old goats died. Only two remained in the enclosure.

"Two goats, six chickens, a few potatoes, and a lot of tobacco leaves," Luis counted.

"We won't last the summer," said Angel.

Paolo turned to Luis. "You have some money, don't you?" he asked.

"I told you: I have a lot. It's in a bank account in Valparaiso. But what good is it? There is nothing to buy here."

"Here, no . . . ," Paolo admitted.

Angel and Luis sighed in unison. Of course, they were not going to let themselves starve in this forlorn house. Of course, a solution had to be found. But all the same . . .

"I've never been to a fair," Paolo said.

"Neither have I," Luis answered.

He knew only the wealthy areas of Valparaiso, the restaurants, the theaters, the bookstores. Not the fairs.

"Is that really what you want?" Angel asked. His heart pounded in his chest. Lately, it had been giving him trouble. It would swell inordinately or rattle like a monkey wanting to escape its cage. All this activity in his chest upset and baffled him. "Is it really what you want?" he insisted.

"It is," said Paolo.

"Yes," added Luis.

Angel shivered. Paolo's words sounded like a knell on

an autumn Sunday. Everything he feared was happening, and he did not see how he could prevent it. If he had had the courage, he would have killed everyone, himself included, to stop time and avoid the suffering he saw coming. But he turned pale at the very idea of taking out his knife. This tool was now good only to peel potatoes.

The next day, they gathered their sparse clothes, and Paolo hooked the shutter of the window. Then he closed the door.

It was a windless, rainless, and sunless morning. The clouds formed a thick, still mass that seemed to crush the earth. Paolo took a last tour of the garden, walked down the path, stroked the mound of dirt with his hand, murmured something, then turned south. Of common accord, Luis and Angel had decided to take that direction. North was not to their liking. North meant Valparaiso and the friends waiting for unlikely letters; north meant Temuco, the police, an unpleasant past from which it was better to keep a distance. For Paolo, any direction was fine. He was leaving his past here, in the center of everything on this desolate land.

"Let's go," he said.

Luis took his bag, just in case. Angel took his knife, just in case. And Paolo took a handful of dirt, which he put in his pocket.

CHAPTER EIGHT

THE FIRST PERSON they met was an alpinist. A Belgian alpinist in search of mountains.

"You're in the right place," Luis told him.

"I prepared my trip carefully," the Belgian explained.

He had rented a donkey in Puerto Natales, and had loaded its back with bags containing enough provisions and gear to face the toughness of the mountain for at least fifteen days.

"Want to see?"

He proudly exhibited his survival kit, his dehydrated soups, his thermal containers; then he started to unpack his brand-new climbing equipment, which consisted of cross belts, ropes, pegs, shoes, thermal blankets, and more.

"I've been dreaming about this for ten years." He laughed, his face gleaming. "So, you can imagine, I had plenty of time to do my shopping."

He stopped laughing when he realized that his listeners did not seem in the mood to chat. The stouter man, in particular, made him uncomfortable. But the man was Chilean! And everyone had praised the hospitality, the easygoing way and generosity of Chileans.

"I have to continue on the road," he said as he started to pack his belongings in a hurry.

In doing so, he turned his back on Angel.

❖

The second person they met was a horseman, a farmer of the Pampas, proud and haughty, who had a dozen fat lambs in his herd.

"Hello!" Angel shouted.

The farmer brought his horse to a halt and whistled to his dog. The lambs, in turn, stopped to nibble on the short grass.

"We are going to Punta Arenas," Angel explained to the rider. "Is this the right way?"

The farmer gave a hard look at the strange party before him. He nodded.

"Is it still far?" Paolo asked.

"Very far," the farmer answered. "I'm headed that way."

Angel told him that they were having a problem with their donkey. "It's limping. Would you be kind enough to take a look? It's the left hind leg."

The farmer was knowledgeable in matters of horses. He came down from his mount, entrusted the bridle to Paolo, and leaned over to examine the leg of the donkey.

In doing so, he turned his back on Angel.

❖

"It wasn't nice to do that," Luis said after a long silence.

He was sitting behind Angel on the horse's back. Around them, heavy clouds were darkening the sky.

Luis shook his head. "No, really, it wasn't—"

Angel pulled on the bridle of the horse abruptly, bringing it to a stop, and Luis couldn't finish his sentence.

"If you want to walk to Punta Arenas, nobody is keeping you," Angel said. "You can get off."

Luis didn't reply. Although he disapproved of the way Angel had plundered the two travelers, he was glad to spare himself the effort of a long walk. But, still, robbery was robbery.

"What is Paolo going to think?" he whispered in Angel's ear. "You're not setting a good example for the child."

Angel shrugged. For once, he had not killed anyone. He had just put the tip of his knife on the napes of the two men to scare them. What was wrong with that? Moreover, he

had bound them neatly, thanks to the brand-new equipment of the Belgian. His only remorse was for the farmer's
dog; it had been too aggressive and had to be destroyed.
Paolo had run after the sheep, which had been scared off by
the gunfire, but had been unable to catch even one.

"It could have turned ugly," Luis continued. "If the
farmer had gotten hold of his rifle—"

"But he didn't. So stop whining. You're getting on my
nerves."

Luis kept quiet. The rifle was swinging in its sheath
against the side of the horse, and at any moment, Angel
could reach for it. Luis exhaled a long and resigned sigh.
While Angel guided the horse over the difficult path, he
thought about the alpinist's threats. "I will complain to my
embassy! I will find you!" the Belgian had shouted. But by
now his furious rantings had long been covered by the gusts
of wind sweeping the plain.

"Maybe we'll be sorry we spared them," Angel muttered
as he thought about the same thing.

Luis felt a long shiver run down his back. Angel did not
seem to be joking. Did that mean he was the kind of man
for whom life had no value? Luis couldn't believe that he
was riding in the company of a murderer, especially after
having seen Angel cry. Nevertheless, he decided to be on
his guard.

Next to them, Paolo was riding on the donkey. He kept
his back straight, his gaze fixed in front of him. The posture
of the farmer had impressed Paolo and he was trying to imi-

tate him. He rode silently, allowing himself to daydream about the landscape, the wind, the comfort of the evening shelter to come, and the smell of soup filling the air. Nothing that Angel had done earlier had shocked him. He was unaware of the laws and commandments of morality; no one had taught him that robbing and roping people was not done. For the first time in his life, he was expecting something from the future. He looked forward to the fair, the city, the cows and the sheep. In front of him, Chile seemed to have spread a ceremonial red carpet. When he reached Punta Arenas, proud and straight on his mount, he was sure it would be a triumph.

CHAPTER NINE

IT TOOK THEM three days to reach the city. Three days to go across changing landscapes, mountains, turbulent streams; three days to endure the cold weather; three days to develop painful saddle sores; three silent days during which each one of them lived like a hermit crab, locked in his own shell.

When they finally reached Punta Arenas, they were so exhausted, they could hardly stay on their mounts. They swayed, sagged, and grimaced with pain at the least jerk of their horse and donkey. Their arrival in Punta Arenas was far from triumphal.

Being penniless, they went straight to the bank to withdraw Luis's money.

"You should wait for us outside," Luis suggested to Angel.

"Why?"

"To keep an eye on the animals."

"I'm no stable boy," Angel grumbled.

Luis passed his fingers through Paolo's hair.

"Listen . . . I really think it would be better if I went in with the child only. It looks more respectable."

Angel frowned, gritting his teeth.

"It's a bank, damn it!" Luis blew up. "A place under electronic surveillance!"

Angel glanced suspiciously at the building. It was gray, cubelike and without charm. A camera above the entrance kept an eye on patrons like a sentry. Angel thought about his knife and about all he had done with it. Would it show? Would the camera see through him and guess what he really was?

"All right," he said, "but Paolo stays with me."

"No, he'll come with me."

"He'll stay outside!"

"He'll come with me!"

"He'll stay out!"

Paolo took Luis's hand. "I've never been inside a bank," he said.

Angel felt his heart shrink to the size of a raisin. He wondered what game Luis was playing. What did he mean that it looked more respectable to go into the bank with a child? Was he going to say to the teller that Paolo was his son? Was he going to ask the child to call him Papa? Was he going to rob Angel of the child's love and tenderness, of the strange happiness that gave meaning to his existence?

Luis knelt in front of the child and tried to fix his hair. He pulled up the collar of his shirt and brushed the sleeves of his coat. The dust made Paolo sneeze. Luis gave him his handkerchief, a square piece of linen as white as snow.

"Hmmm," he said, getting up. "It'll be okay."

Finally, Angel let them both enter the bank, hand in hand. He remained alone, bareheaded, under the newly falling rain.

Inside the bank, Paolo took off the gloves he had found among the alpinist's belongings, and soon the warmth of the place made him mellow. People were coming and going, and waiting patiently in lines in front of the tellers' booths. There were city men in dark suits, seamen in yellow slickers, men from the Pampas in leather coats, and women. It had been a very, very long time since Paolo had seen a woman—since the death of his mother—and he was looking at them with intense curiosity. Some of the bank employees wore skirts and high-heeled shoes. Paolo noticed that Luis was also looking at the women, that he was watching them with great attention.

They entered the line facing the withdrawal counter. After so much time spent in the desolate house, and after three days on the road, being in a bank was strange. You couldn't hear the rain or wind, only the sound of voices, the clatter of machines, and the ringing of phones. Behind the tinted windows, the outside world seemed unreal. Paolo had never walked on a carpeted floor before, and he wanted to remove his shoes to feel the softness under his feet. Compared to his world of rocks, dirt, and wind, the bank was like a calm, padded, civilized universe. It was as if he had crossed time and space and arrived on another planet. Yet he was not afraid. Luis's presence reassured him: Luis, at least, knew city ways and could be trusted.

When they reached the counter, Paolo went on tiptoe to see what was behind it. A gray-haired woman smiled kindly at him, then asked Luis what he wanted. Luis opened his bag and took out his wallet. He showed his identity card to the woman. She turned to her computer, smiled again, and asked Luis to fill out a form. Meanwhile, Paolo admired the potted plants, the clock on the wall, the filing cabinets from which employees removed papers they distributed to clients. Here, no one was chasing snakes, no knife was to be seen, and no chicken was being plucked. There was even a water fountain with plastic cups. Paolo observed people as they said "hello" or "goodbye" or "how are you" to one another. Everything seemed so simple and pleasant.

Then the teller handed a bundle of brand-new bills to Luis over the counter.

"Would your son like a sweet?" she asked.

"Do you want one, Paolo?" said Luis.

Paolo nodded. He did not know what a sweet was but

was ready to take anything this nice lady wanted to give him. She held out a basket. He looked at the different-colored wrappers and chose a yellow one.

The lady smiled again. "I prefer the yellow ones too!" she said, giving Paolo a warm and tender grandmotherly look.

It was time to go. Reluctantly Paolo buttoned his coat and pulled his head down into his shoulders. On his way out, he squeezed the sweet—now his talisman—determined to keep it all his life. The yellow paper, like a small piece of sun fallen from the sky, could only bring him luck.

CHAPTER TEN

THE CATTLE FAIR was to be held the day after next. Luis's money would be enough to cover lodging and eating expenses until then. There would even be enough left to buy some sheep, as well as a cow.

Luis was told of an inn that would accommodate their mounts, and where two rooms with sinks could be had at a reasonable price. They went there at sunset, under the rain. Angel was still upset with Luis about the bank and kept silent, making sure to guide his horse into every rut and pothole on the road. With each jolt, Luis moaned in pain.

The inn looked like a cutthroat place. Its pitched roof came down to meet small and dirty windows, which were never opened and which were rotting inside because of the condensation. A smell of wet dog and human sweat greeted Angel and Luis as they walked in, a smell strong enough to wipe out their appetite. Maybe that was just as well, considering the quality of the food. The innkeeper, a small and skinny man with a yellowing beard, chewed on an old pipe as he showed them the rooms. Meanwhile, Paolo had taken the horse and donkey to the back of the inn, where a canopy functioned as a stable. A mixture of mud and dung stuck to the soles of his shoes. As he waded through the filth, he thought about the bank and the sweet, and wondered why anyone had to live in a place like the inn when there were lots of heated houses with carpeting.

In the dining hall, the innkeeper's wife served them a mutton stew that was too salty and a pitcher of wine that had been diluted with water. The greasy tables were riddled with holes, the chairs were wobbly, the fireplace was sooty, and thick smoke hung above the guests' heads like fog coming from the sea. Since they had gotten only two rooms for three people, how to split them was a problem. With whom would Paolo sleep?

"He'll sleep with me," Angel declared. "I'm his father."

"My room seems warmer," Luis objected.

"But it's smaller."

"I think I noticed that your sink was clogged."

"Paolo doesn't need to wash himself."

As he chewed on the stew, Paolo looked at the pictures hanging on the walls of the room. The paintings depicted life in Punta Arenas: a trawler in the harbor, people coming out of church on a sunny day, a farmers' market. Paolo thought the pictures were pretty; he liked the colors. He got up and approached the one showing the scene of the harbor. He reached out with his hand to feel the surface.

"Don't touch that!" the innkeeper shouted from the other end of the room.

Startled, Paolo put his hand in his pocket. The innkeeper came toward him.

"Do you like it?" the man asked.

Paolo looked at him. "I've never seen . . . ," he started saying.

"You've never seen a painting?"

Paolo shook his head. The man was eyeing him in a friendly way.

"My daughter, Delia, painted them." The innkeeper turned to Luis and Angel. "They're for sale, if you're interested."

Luis got up and went to Paolo's side. He looked at the painting more closely.

"Do you like it?" Luis asked.

"Yes," Paolo whispered.

Luis turned to the innkeeper. "How much?"

The man motioned for him to wait. He crossed the room and disappeared behind a small door. Now Angel got up; he could feel complications coming on.

"You're proud of your money, aren't you?" he said to Luis.

"I'm not proud of it," Luis answered quietly. "I use it, that's all."

The innkeeper returned a few minutes later, accompanied by a young woman.

"This is my daughter, Delia."

The young girl came forward shyly. She wore overalls made of thick material, and a shawl was thrown around her shoulders. Her thick black hair was held back by a comb and her bright face had the softness of dawn.

"Is it for you?" she asked Paolo gently.

Paolo remained silent.

"Yes," Luis answered in his place. "I want to give him a present."

"Nothing is decided yet," said Angel.

The young woman turned her face toward the one who had spoken in a harsh voice. The murderer swallowed with difficulty.

"Sit down!" the innkeeper suggested. "I will treat you to a bottle of my personal reserve."

The four of them sat at the table. Paolo faced Delia, and next to him Luis faced Angel, who poured more wine than was reasonable. The young woman spoke eagerly about her paintings, the colors of the town, her walks, and the way she chose her subjects.

"I wanted to register at the School of Fine Arts in Santiago. But this involves a trip by train, a room to rent, and supplies to buy. We are not rich enough. So I try to save money from the paintings I sell. Once a week, I rent a stand at the market. Sometimes a tourist buys one or two of my canvases. At the inn, they are more for decoration. Farmers don't pay much attention to art." Her eyes met those of Paolo. "Fortunately, there are a few sensitive children who have a good eye." She smiled at him.

Luis started to talk earnestly of the Valparaiso museums, mentioning the names of famous artists, making long and complicated sentences. He paused, looking for the right words, citing dates, getting enthusiastic about colors with unfamiliar names. These made Paolo's imagination go wild: vermilion, carmine, Prussian blue, ochre, emerald green. . . . Delia too became excited, and her and Luis's words danced in Paolo's ears. His jaw tight, Angel grew impatient.

"Would you like some more wine?" he asked Delia.

"With pleasure."

Paolo saw Angel's hand briefly touch that of the young woman and noticed that he spilled some of the wine.

"I will buy the painting of the harbor," Luis decided. "Your price will be mine."

Delia looked at Paolo again. "You're lucky," she said, "to have such a nice father."

Angel opened his mouth to answer, but Paolo was faster than he was.

"Luis is not my father," he explained.

The young woman raised her eyebrows and turned to

Angel. It seemed impossible that this man, with his thick neck and rough hands, could be the father of such a sensitive child. Angel could sense the feeling of suspicion and distrust hanging over him. Right away, he wanted to flee this place, but he forced himself to stay put.

Delia got up and went to take the painting down.

"How old are you?" she asked Paolo.

"I don't know."

"And your first name?" she said, laughing. "Do you know it?"

"Paolo. Paolo Poloverdo."

She turned the painting over on her knees and took a pen out of one of her overall pockets. *For the shining eyes of Paolo Poloverdo, one evening, in Punta Arenas*, she wrote on the back. Then she handed the canvas to the child.

Luis told Delia that he did not want to take out his money in front of the other guests in the dining hall. He suggested that she accompany him to his room. Delia nodded. Her cheeks were flushed, and the air was so charged with electricity that Paolo could feel tingles on the back of his neck.

Luis took Delia's hand, then turned to Angel, who remained frozen in his chair, his face tense.

"It's agreed," Luis said. "Paolo will sleep with you."

CHAPTER ELEVEN

THAT NIGHT, ANGEL was unable to sleep. He tried to think of ways to get rid of Luis, but nothing short of killing him came to mind, and this was upsetting. Between two flashes of anger, he listened to Paolo's breathing. The child's breath acted like a poultice on his enraged feelings. Then he thought of Delia's lovely face, her hair, her burning eyes, and once more choked with rage.

Angel put his boots on and went out. What time could it be? There was no noise in the corridor. He put his ear against Luis's door and heard nothing. The silence was worse than anything else. Each step of the stairway creaked as Angel went down. He opened the front door and let the cold wind whip his face. He could feel a wave of pain and violence come over him, an enormous wave that his body was unable to contain. He went out into the damp night.

As he walked toward the center of town, he had the impression of walking in a dream. Moments of his life rushed to his mind: he remembered the other cities, Talcahuano and Temuco, the neon lights of bars, the fights, the blows, the fear, the hatred, and the repugnance. He started to run. At the end of the street, he could see lights. They were waving in front of his eyes; Angel was intoxicated with pain.

The bar he entered was crowded. Young men and women were laughing and dancing among the tables. They were celebrating the departure of a fishing boat, which was to weigh anchor at sunrise. The men, their faces reddened with excitement, were going to spend weeks at sea, deprived of everything, completely at the mercy of the ocean. It was as if they could hear death knocking on their door, so they drank and danced all the more. Unaware of how it happened, Angel found himself with a mug of beer in his hands, then another, and another. He started to laugh and dance like the others, but felt that he was no longer himself. It was almost as if his body were in the bar while his soul waited outside. And as he danced, he felt his knife knock against his chest like a second beating heart.

Later, as he slumped on a bench, a drunken girl fell asleep against him, her head on his shoulder. She smelled of tobacco, alcohol, and sweat. He shook her. In her blurry eyes, he saw his reflection: his chiseled face, his dirty beard, and the grin of a man consumed by madness. A flash went through him. He lifted the girl's head to his mouth—to kiss or bite her, he no longer knew. Around them, the jubilant crowd turned round and round in a frenzied circle. Angel felt his arms lose their strength. The girl slid down against the back of the bench onto the dirty floor. She was laughing and talking, but Angel understood nothing of what she said. He got up and put the palms of his hands on the wall to catch his breath. Under him, he could see the girl, breathing. She had gone back to sleep. Angel's throat tightened. No, this time he did not want this girl. Or Delia. Or any other.

He got up and elbowed his way through the crowd of revelers.

For the rest of the night he walked the streets around the harbor, with no idea of the time, simply spitting and shouting into the darkness. He was sick of himself and of the world. More than anything, he badly wanted to be someone else!

Finally, as the sun began to peek through the sky, he stopped. A ray of vivid light colored the surface of the sea. He felt cold and aware that his fever had subsided. He shook himself and decided to go back to the inn. Paolo would be waking up soon. What would he think if he found himself all alone? Abandoned, that was what!

Angel started to run through town. He inhaled the crisp early-morning air and exhaled all the hatred and violence left within him.

When he entered his room at the inn, he was glad to see Paolo sleeping calmly, curled up in the middle of the bed. He sat on the side of the mattress and stroked the child's forehead very gently with the tips of his fingers. He stayed like this for an hour, not moving, with the impression that he was finally absorbing the meaning of life. The shy birth of dawn, the breath of a sleeping child, and a man with the huge hands of a killer, seated in the dark, suffering: that was life.

CHAPTER TWELVE

PAOLO AWOKE, DISTURBED by something heavy on his legs. He sat up and saw Angel lying across the bed, fully dressed, his body weighing on Paolo's legs. Paolo freed himself and bent over the face of the man. He felt his warm breath and was reassured. In the daze of waking up, he had thought that Angel had been overcome by a mysterious force and had died. He pushed the blankets away and got out of bed. As he put his clothes on, he contemplated the painting that he had placed on the dresser. The harbor, the boat, the yellow spots of the slickers, the sea. He squinted and had the feeling that he was entering the picture. He could smell the fish. His heart swelled like a sponge and something trembled deep in his body. It was both an upsetting and an immensely pleasant feeling.

Angel was snoring on the bed as Paolo left the room.

Paolo did not find Luis downstairs and did not dare to knock on his door. Instead, he decided to tend to the donkey and horse: after all, the animals were just as worthy as the two men.

An overcast day had risen on the muddy backyard. Paolo hopped over puddles to reach the canopy where the animals were prancing with hunger, their fur wet and shining. He found some hay at the back of the shelter and sat on an old saddle to watch them eat. Behind him, attached to rusty nails, was a lot of equipment forgotten by strangers passing through: saddle covers, straps, currycombs, halters. . . . Paolo got hold of a leather riding whip and hit the ground with it, making the straw fly around. Then he made marks in the loamy soil with the tip of the whip. At first, he drew all sorts of lines. Then he discovered that the whip was flexible, and he came down from the saddle to pay more attention to what he was doing. Words took shape in the mud, almost more easily than on Luis's white sheets of paper: *Paolo—Chile—fox—knife—pitcher*. He considered the result. After thinking it over, he traced a *P*, followed by an *I, K, S, U, R, E. PIKSURE.*

The child was startled when he saw Delia approach, and his face reddened. He trampled over the mud to erase the words he had just written and quickly covered the spot with straw. Wrapped in her shawl, Delia came to him under the canopy. She stroked the neck of the donkey, then that of the horse.

"Are they yours?" she asked.

"Yes."

"You take good care of them, I see."

"Yes."

She crouched in front of him. "I hear that you came to Punta Arenas for the cattle fair."

"Yes."

"Which one is really your father? Luis or Angel?"

Paolo frowned and lowered his head. What was the answer? Neither man was his real father, but how was he to decide? Angel had taken care of him, fed him, and given him the fox. Luis had taught him the alphabet and the beauty of poems, and had given him the painting. Both men made him suffer and live at the same time, just as fathers do. Delia guessed his embarrassment and changed the subject.

"How many lambs would you like to buy?"

"I don't know."

"Ten?"

"Yes."

"You need a lot of money for ten lambs!"

"And also a cow!"

"Luis is really rich, then?"

"Very. He goes to the bank and asks a nice lady for money. She gives him bills. She gave me . . ."

Paolo stopped. He did not feel like talking about the sweet, his talisman. He feared that to reveal its existence would break its magical power.

"She gave you what?"

"Nothing. A glass of water."

Delia laughed. "You're a funny boy!"

She passed her cool hand through Paolo's unkempt hair and gathered him in her arms. Then she kissed his cheek. Just as quickly, she crossed the yard to go back to the inn. Seeing her go, Paolo felt overcome by a sadness that he had never felt before, even when thinking about his dead mother under the mound. It was a deep, strong sadness—one that encompassed a very private and important truth. He looked at the whip that he still held in his hand. The words *pitcher, Chile,* even *piksure* could not express his feelings.

❖

When he woke up, Angel noticed that Paolo was no longer in the bed, and it was he who felt totally abandoned. He opened the tap of the sink, splashed water over his face, and looked at himself in the rust-spotted mirror. Did he deserve to live? he wondered. He was going to be thirty-seven, the very age his father had been when he had died of tuberculosis. Angel put a hand on his chest. Weren't his lungs on fire too? Wouldn't it be fair if he died, even if his death did not avenge all those he had killed? Tuberculosis was a filthy disease. He had been five when his father had convulsed with pain and spat up black blood. Ever since, the smell of blood had stayed with him.

While he had been sleeping, Paolo had left. With Luis? With Luis and Delia? If that was the case, he would make sure to die this very day, because his life would be unbearable.

He dried his face with the back of his sleeve and walked out of the room. There was no one in the corridor, but he could hear whispers and laughter coming from Luis's room. He knocked on the door.

"Who is it?"

"Angel!"

"One minute!"

He heard muffled noises and steps. Then Luis appeared at the door, his hair disheveled.

"Where's Paolo?" Angel asked.

"I don't know."

"I saw him with the horses under the canopy," Delia said behind Luis.

Angel looked into Luis's eyes. Unexpectedly, he smiled. Luis did not understand the meaning of this smile, but for Angel it signaled the beginning of a beautiful day. It was one more day to live and spend with Paolo, who was waiting for him under the canopy. It did not matter that Luis had spent the night with Delia; the happiness of others was not important.

"Give me some money," he said. "I want to take the child to the harbor and treat him to a good meal."

Luis nodded and pushed the door closed before returning with two bills.

"Treat yourself too," he said, handing the money to Angel. "As for me, I buy paintings." He winked.

"Thanks," said Angel.

He turned on his heels and went down the stairs, making each step creak. He no longer felt jealous. Delia could do whatever she wanted. Luis could open a museum. He didn't care. Paolo had not abandoned him. He had only risen early.

But Paolo was not under the canopy, and the donkey had disappeared. Suddenly Angel felt as if someone had plunged a knife into his stomach. Paolo *had* left! Why? What had happened? What foolish idea had come to the child's mind? Angel rushed over to the horse and rode off at a gallop. The donkey's hoofs had left some mud traces on the pavement, but not enough to guide Angel in a precise direction. Instinctively, Angel headed straight for the harbor. He was beginning to understand Paolo's ways. He needed to look for him where the trawlers came and went, where the artists painted them.

CHAPTER THIRTEEN

CONTRARY TO WHAT Angel thought, Paolo had not gone to the harbor. He had headed east of town, following a rocky path that reminded him of the one that led to his house. But this path didn't lead to a windy and desolate expanse of land. It ended at the top of cliffs overlooking the Strait of Magellan.

The donkey was tired. Paolo stuck the bridle between two rocks. His heart was anguished by many strange feelings, and he went near the edge of the cliff to contemplate the sea.

Things happen when you watch the sea for long periods of time. And gradually, as Paolo observed the waves, spume, and birds flying against the wind, his body began to feel weightless, as if he were floating between the sky and the earth, as light as a snowflake. He could almost feel the swell of the sea, the rip currents, and when he looked down the cliff, he had the impression of crashing against the rocks, of becoming a wave. Only his hands resting on the moss kept him in touch with the planet. He had never studied geography, geology, or astronomy, but he could clearly see his role in the universe, as if a veil had been lifted, and the truth revealed.

He thought about his birth and the narrow passageway he must have opened in his mother's belly. With each breath he took, he felt he was tasting the air for the first time. He could hear himself uttering his first cry as a newborn, a cry that was in answer to all the cries given from the beginning of time, by all the generations of human beings.

What had become of these millions of babies? Some had died, others had grown up. Among them, there had been beggars, kings, sailors, and farmers; some had fought proudly with their conquistadores' swords; others had shaken with fear and surrendered, kneeling on the ground and the ashes of their homes as they prayed madly to God, or gently like wounded poets. All this humanity was churning in Paolo before the sad truth of what was breaking his heart became obvious to him: he missed the love of a mother.

He cried, alone, facing the sea.

He cried a long time.

And he cried some more.

The wind dried his tears and made white furrows on his skin. It wasn't so much the death of his mother that made him cry as the fact that he could not remember if she had ever kissed his cheek. He couldn't remember if he had ever felt from her the warmth that he had experienced when Delia had taken him in her arms. How had he been able to live without this warmth?

Behind him, the donkey brayed.

Paolo spat into the sea.

CHAPTER FOURTEEN

THE HORSE'S HOOVES pounded on the asphalt and its nostrils were dilated; Angel stood up in the stirrups shouting Paolo's name. He could see nothing but spots of colors and blurred shapes fleeing in front of him.

"Crazy horseman! Crazy horseman!" the people yelled.

Angel and his horse plowed their way through the crowd. They rushed toward the boats, jumped over moorings and stacks of barrels, scattered groups of fishermen and crates of fish. It was hard to distinguish who was neighing: the man or the horse. Both had feverish eyes.

"Call the police!" a woman shouted.

"And the loony bin!" added another.

With each leap of the horse, Angel's coattails went flying around him. He looked like a specter, a sorrowful creature who had come from some lost world.

At last, the specter reached the end of the wharf. The horse reared in front of the sea. Again, the man shouted a name. "*Paolo!*" Behind him, the people in the harbor were recovering from their bewilderment. Such a spectacle had never been seen before. The police had to be alerted.

While phone lines started to buzz, Angel disappeared. But when the police arrived at the harbor, several onlookers gave concurring descriptions of the horseman, so it was going to be easy to make a composite sketch. Had this man damaged anything? the police inquired. Yes. He had overturned a few fish crates and crushed some dead fish. Had this man hurt anyone? Yes. He had caused a frightened fisherman to fall into the cold and dirty waters of the harbor. As a measure of precaution, the police researched the records of other provinces and communicated the madman's profile as far as Santiago.

❖

Angel had left at full gallop on his horse, his eyes filled with tears. He sped along the shore, on paved roads, then on wild paths where the wind played with the grass. All the while he shouted Paolo's name. Anything could have happened to him!

"*Paolo-o! Paolo-o!*"

Suddenly, Angel saw the donkey browsing at the edge of a cliff. He pulled on the horse's bridle to slow it down. His heart stopped beating. He couldn't see the child. One step at a time, slowly, slowly, good. He didn't want to scare him.

As he rounded a thorny bush, he spotted Paolo's small body right behind the donkey. Angel's heart started to beat again. But what was Paolo doing seated at the edge of the cliff? As silent as a snake, Angel got off his horse and moved toward the child. The wind was whistling in his ears. It was fiercely cold. The vast sea spread out in front of him, and the cliff seemed to be pitching like a ship in distress.

"Paolo," Angel whispered.

The child looked over his shoulder. Two or three meters separated them.

"I'm going to jump," Paolo said.

Angel held back a scream. Already, small stones were crumbling under the fingers of the crying child. It would take very little to make him fall down the cliff.

"Why do you want to jump?" Angel asked.

"I want to die."

"Why do you want to die?"

Paolo did not answer and turned his head toward the sea. Angel took a cautious step forward like someone playing Red Light, Green Light. Then he stopped, realizing just how fragile was the thread that linked the child to this world.

"May I come next to you?" he asked.

"No, you're going to keep me from jumping."

"Why would I do that?"

Paolo looked at Angel.

"In your opinion," Angel went on, "why would I prevent you from jumping?"

"Because . . ." The donkey twitched his ears. "Because you do all you can to annoy me," Paolo finally said.

"That's not the real reason."

"Oh, no? So why did you kill my parents? Why did you come to my house? Why did you give me a fox?"

Angel tried to think fast.

"I did all that, it's true," he said. "Why? Because I'm clumsy."

The trace of a smile came over the child's lips. "Very clumsy," he agreed. Then his mood darkened again. "I'm going to jump now."

"Wait! I'm not finished talking."

The horse blew air through his nostrils. Birds cried out in the sky, high above them. Between two clouds the moon was visible, even though it was broad daylight.

"Luis gave me some money," Angel said. "One bill for you, one for me. Why don't we go eat a good meal in town?"

"I'm not hungry."

"We could look at the shops, at the boats, dream about another life."

"I'm not—"

"Wait!" Angel cut him short. "Here's what I want to tell you. It's the real reason I looked for you in the harbor and shouted your name all over town. Do you know why?"

Paolo curled his fingers and felt gravel lodge under his nails.

"Because you love me?" he asked.

"Yes."

Angel had managed to come closer. Only one meter separated them now. He could see Paolo's red eyes and tearstained cheeks.

"Do you really love me?" the child asked.

"Yes."

Angel saw the child push against the cliff with his legs. He saw his bottom rise and his body tip over. Angel screamed and threw himself forward.

There was a jumble of arms, legs, kicks, stones, blows, and shouts. Angel had closed his arms around Paolo's thin chest and held him tight. All his strength was concentrated in his arms. He crawled back, far from the edge, the child fighting him. Even once the danger of the cliff was gone, Angel kept his hold around Paolo's shoulders. Their eyes met.

"But you'll never be my mother," Paolo whispered.

"That's true," Angel answered.

He sat on the ground, lifted the child onto his lap, and cradled him, slowly rocking back and forth. Without thinking, he started to sing. He didn't know how the song came to his lips—whether his own mother had sung it to him when he was too young to realize she was dying, or whether he had heard it through an open window and stolen it like everything else. It didn't matter, though. He was singing for

Paolo with the sincerity of someone who has never sung before and whose voice rises suddenly, out of necessity, with the only purpose to comfort.

"I'm just a murderer," Angel whispered, "but I know one thing. When you're sad and have the good fortune to find a shoulder to cry on, you shouldn't hesitate." He tightened his embrace. "Cry," he added.

And so Paolo cried. He could feel the sweet, his talisman, stuck in the fold of his pants pocket, pressing against his thigh as if to prove to him that he was truly alive.

CHAPTER FIFTEEN

IT WAS ALMOST twilight when Angel and Paolo returned to the inn. Their bellies were full, their hands frozen, their eyes shining, and their hearts as raw as a fresh skin wound. In the dining hall, the tables had been set for dinner with worn and stained checkered tablecloths, soup bowls, and pitchers of red wine. Indifferent to the smell of sautéing onions wafting into the room, Delia and Luis were kissing near the fireplace, holding hands.

"I was beginning to worry about you," Luis called out to them.

"I can see that," Angel said, taking off his coat.

"Come over here, Paolo," Luis said, beckoning to him.

The child went shyly near the fire. He did not dare look at Delia, afraid that her eyes would glitter with that particular love shared only by adults. He feared it would spoil the memory of the almost motherly hug and kiss that had troubled him so deeply.

"Did Angel take good care of you?" Luis asked.

"Yes."

"Did you see the boats?"

"Yes. B-o-t-e-s."

A large smile came over Luis's face. "Very good, very good indeed!"

Delia was laughing. Paolo almost looked at her but checked himself.

"It's not quite the way to spell *boat*," Luis explained, "but who cares? The important thing is that I understood what you meant, right? Let's have a drink."

Delia got up to fetch glasses and a bottle of wine from the kitchen, and Luis made Paolo sit on his lap.

"Tomorrow is the big day. We'll go to the fair very early. It will still be dark. But you'll get to see the best cattle sold before noon."

Paolo got off Luis's lap when he heard Delia coming back. He wondered what was going to happen once the fair was over. Would Delia be coming to live with them in the forlorn house? It would mean having to buy another horse, and crowding a little more to sleep.

The four of them sat around a table and poured wine into the glasses. Even Paolo was given some. Gradually he loosened up. His body filled with warmth and he leaned against Angel's chest. The murderer did not seem as sullen this evening. In fact, he was laughing and clinking glasses. The innkeeper joined them and told innkeeper stories. In the thirty years he had run this place in Punta Arenas, he said, he had seen many characters. It was from Punta Arenas that adventurers set out on expeditions: seafaring people who sailed or rowed, skydivers, waterskiing buffs, all of them fascinated by this part of the world and willing to risk their lives and savings to realize their dreams.

The innkeeper became animated and chewed on his pipe. The onion smell was getting stronger, indicating that the soup was almost ready. The man told them that when adventurers got lost, the police asked Delia to draw the missing person's portrait in charcoal. This work helped to butter the bread; and thanks to Delia's drawings, many of these adventurers had been saved.

Cozy in his comfort, Paolo was falling asleep in his chair. He shivered from time to time, remembering that he had almost died that very morning. He had made Angel swear that he would not talk to anyone about what had happened. The words they had said to each other on the cliff's edge would remain buried within them forever. Just as the Poloverdos and the fox were. When he made the promise, Angel had smiled: all these secrets were beginning to establish a serious link between the two of them. A link that a father and son would share, or, at the very least . . . friends.

❖

The next morning Paolo was awakened by Angel's cool, large hands on his forehead. It was time to go to the cattle market.

"Pack your belongings," Angel advised. "We won't be coming back to the inn."

"Are we leaving right afterward?"

"Yes."

"With our sheep and our cow?"

"Absolutely."

"And Luis?"

Angel shrugged.

"And Delia?"

"Dress quickly, please."

The child obeyed. He wrapped Delia's painting in the raincoat that Angel had brought with him, felt his pants pocket to make sure that the sweet was still there, and waited by the door. He watched as Angel tidied up the room, first wiping the sink with a sponge, then straightening the sheets and blankets on the bed. Although he did not know why, Paolo sensed that this was a very important moment in his life. Later, whenever he would impatiently wait for something, he always remembered this sound of sheets being straightened and the lingering smell of onions.

In turn, Luis and Delia came tiptoeing out into the corridor. They did not look too good, no doubt due to lack of sleep. Downstairs the four of them drank some warm milk; then they buttoned their coats.

"Let's go," Angel muttered.

They left the muddy courtyard and fetched the animals. None of them turned for a farewell look at the pitched roof and dirty windows of the inn. Not even Paolo, who was conscious of leaving something behind. And not Delia, who had packed her art supplies, as well as a large bag, all of which burdened the donkey's back.

CHAPTER SIXTEEN

THERE WAS A crowd under the market roof. Farmers from Argentina had come from nearby Patagonia with their sheep, cows, dogs, wives, and children, and everyone was camping like refugees. They warmed their hands around the braziers, drank strong coffee, and were already discussing prices. The youngsters were still sleeping in the stacks of straw, all curled up and huddled together under the vigilant gaze of the women.

Some less fortunate farmers were selling their cattle just outside the market. This created total chaos, in spite of the fences and the warnings from the organizers.

Once the donkey and horse had been secured in a temporary box at the end of the street, Angel and Paolo weaved their way into the market. They had agreed to meet up with Luis and Delia later on to talk about their first impressions and to discuss eventual purchases.

"Ten sheep and a cow," Paolo reminded Luis.

"Yes, yes," Luis muttered. "We'll see."

Paolo held on to Angel's hand. Paolo was moving like a sleepwalker in the middle of the rising agitation and shouts of the merchants. So this was what a fair looked like! Half filled with wonder, half scared, Paolo went on tiptoe to catch sight of the bulls. He was used to smaller animals. These muscular beasts left him speechless.

"Would you like us to buy a bull?" Angel asked as he lifted the child onto his shoulders.

From this height, Paolo could see the entire fair. Hundreds of men and heads of cattle billowed in the half-light, as dogs barked, sheep bleated, and merchants shouted and slapped hands with buyers. All this produced a festive uproar.

The change from the money that Luis had given Angel was in Angel's pocket, and the coins jingled as he walked.

"Do you want a pancake?" he asked Paolo.

They made their way to a stall where a large woman wrapped in a poncho was cooking rounds of dough in a dented frying pan. Around her, the smell of hot oil mixed with that of wet straw. Paolo took the pancake in his hands and ate it. It burned his tongue, which amused Angel.

"Now let's move on and give the sheep a closer look," Angel said.

They stopped in front of an enclosure where clean, fat sheep jostled each other. At the far end, the seller was already bargaining with two farmers. Paolo gripped the fence and hoisted himself up to stroke a lamb. Meanwhile, Angel approached the merchant, and the three men not only made way for him but stopped their discussion.

"How much a head?" Angel asked.

"It depends," the seller said.

"We would like ten of them."

"Only ten?"

"Our farm is small," Angel said apologetically.

At that moment, Paolo called out to him.

"I want this one!" he shouted. "Look, we're friends already."

Delighted, the child plunged both hands into the fleece of the gentle lamb. Angel turned back to the merchant. At his side, the two farmers were frowning suspiciously. Suddenly Angel felt his throat tighten. He did not like the look in the eyes of these men.

"Well," he said in a low voice, "we'll come back later." And he hurried toward Paolo. "Come."

"But . . . my lamb?"

"Not now."

"Why?"

"We have to talk to Luis," Angel explained. "Come quickly."

He took Paolo's hand and pushed him ahead as they entered the crowd. Instinctively he pulled the hood of his coat over his head. An old fright had come upon him, much as the body of a drowned man comes back to the surface of a lake. Those looks! How many times had he caught the same flash of suspicion in the eyes of others? Dozens of times! But this had not happened in a long while, not since he had arrived at the Poloverdo house.

"Why are you running?" Paolo asked. "Where are we going?"

Angel had not noticed his quickened pace. They soon found themselves at a square, at the back of the market. The sun had risen and the cloudless sky was shining above the roofs, promising a nice day.

"Oh!" Paolo shouted. "The bank!"

They were opposite the bank building. The day they had arrived, Angel had not noticed the market, as it had been empty and silent. They moved forward, near the few people tapping their feet as they waited for the bank to open. Among them, Angel noticed Luis and Delia, who was carrying the large bag on her back.

"You're here," Luis said, surprised. He seemed upset.

"I saw a lamb," Paolo said with enthusiasm. "We're friends. I'm sure you'll love him too!"

Then he noticed Luis's pale face and realized that something strange was happening. He didn't know why, but he thought Luis seemed afraid. What was there to fear on such a magnificent day as this one?

"Why are you going to the bank?" Angel asked.

"I've—well—I must—" Luis stammered.

Delia took his arm and spoke for him.

"We have to withdraw some more money," she said. "Luis does not have enough to buy ten sheep."

"I hadn't factored in the purchase of the painting, and then the money I gave you yesterday," Luis explained.

Angel remained silent. His hood fell loosely over his eyes, casting a troubling shadow on the top of his face.

"Can I come with you?" Paolo asked Luis.

He was dying to go into the magical bank again. He wanted to feel the carpeting under his feet, and see the water fountain, the clock, all the nice things.

"You know, I won't be but a minute. Delia is coming with me. We shouldn't be so many at the counter. You'll be in the way."

Paolo opened his mouth to protest. He wanted to remind Luis how respectable it was to go into a bank with a child. That was what Luis had said the other day! What was different now? Paolo looked at Delia. Of course, *she* was the difference. . . . But, suddenly, Angel pushed him toward Luis.

"The child wants to go," he said.

"It's not necessary," Luis said again.

Just then, the doors of the bank opened and Paolo caught a glimpse of the gray-haired woman, who was welcoming the first clients with a jovial smile. He wondered if she would offer him another sweet. That would make two talismans!

"Take the child with you," Angel ordered.

Luis sighed and took Paolo's hand.

As they entered the bank, the heat blew on Paolo's face. He smiled. Nothing had changed since two days ago. It was the same peaceful place, the same padded atmosphere that made one feel one was inside a bubble.

Delia and Luis whispered secrets in line. At the counters, other people were also talking softly, and all the hushed tones sounded like the rustling of the wind in the trees.

Paolo pulled on Luis's sleeve. "Do you think I can have a glass of water?"

"Go ahead," said Luis.

Slowly the child went over to the fountain. He admired the pile of cups, the tap, and noticed a pedal at the foot of the machine. He took a cup and pushed on the pedal with his right foot. A clear stream of water ran from the tap. Paolo put his cup under it and waited until it was full. With care, he brought the cup to his lips. He did this a few times with growing pleasure.

In his house at the tip of Chile, water was in short supply. Whenever he saw the bottom of the pitcher, he always hesitated to pour again, because it meant that he would have to go out into the cold, the wind, the rain, and walk to the well and pull on the chain, which hurt his fingers. Here all he had to do was push on the pedal and he could drink until he dropped.

"You should stop, child," a man who was passing near Paolo told him. "This fountain is not a toy."

Paolo blushed. He threw away the cup and joined Luis and Delia. They both had their elbows on the counter and were leaning forward. Paolo pulled on Luis's sleeve.

"What now?" Luis said, out of temper.

"Do you think I'll get another sweet?" Paolo asked.

Luis shrugged and turned away. Abashed, Paolo insinuated himself close to the counter. He wanted to make sure that it was the nice gray-haired lady who was there, but Luis's body hid the teller's face.

"What do you need an authorization for?" Luis was saying tensely. "I'm in a hurry."

"That's the rule for large amounts," the teller answered. "It's the law."

"Very well! Call the bank manager!" Luis said excitedly. Then he felt Paolo between his legs and gave him a nasty look. "Go play somewhere else!"

"The fountain is not a toy," Paolo answered.

"Then go outside with Angel!"

Paolo hung his head down. He did not like the way Luis was speaking, or the way he acted, or looked, or . . . It was Delia's fault. Luis was different since he had met her. With a heavy heart, Paolo went to the exit. This time, he would not be getting a sweet. He felt sad. And when he pushed the door open, tears came to his eyes.

"Where is Luis?" Angel asked.

His throat tight, Paolo did not answer.

"What's the matter?" Angel knelt in front of the child. "You're crying? Is it because of Luis?"

Paolo nodded.

"Is it because Luis no longer wants to buy the sheep?" Angel wiped the tears running down the child's cheeks. "Don't worry, I promised that you would have your lamb. One way or the other, we'll get one, I swear."

Suddenly, Angel saw a change come across Paolo's face. The child's sadness was replaced by a look of astonishment. Paolo's eyes were fixed on a spot above Angel's shoulder. Angel tried to turn around, but Paolo grabbed his face roughly between his hands.

"Don't move," he whispered.

Angel felt his heart stop. Again!

"What do you see?" he asked between clenched teeth.

"Men," Paolo answered.

"What are they doing?"

"They are behind you, near the market entrance."

"What are they doing?" he repeated.

"They're sticking up posters."

Paolo's hands were squeezing Angel's face like a vise, while his anxious eyes followed the movements of the bill stickers.

"What is on the posters?" Angel asked, though deep down, he already knew.

"It's your portrait, Angel. Your picture in charcoal."

CHAPTER SEVENTEEN

THE MAN AND the child exchanged glances. They did not need to say a word to understand each other. Once the bill stickers had gone inside the market, Angel got up slowly and, hand in hand, he and Paolo walked in the direction of the boxes.

Under his hood, Angel was dripping with perspiration. The feeling of danger was suffocating him. In the past, when he knew he was hunted, he had just left town. He acted as a trapped animal would, without thinking. It was, after all, a kind of game. The cops, the thieves ... who would run faster? And even if he had been arrested and sent to jail, what would have been the difference? To live alone, whether free or locked in a prison cell, would be to endure the same suffering. But this time, it was no longer a game.

Angel could feel Paolo's small hand in his, and he knew that he could not bear to have Paolo taken away. As a free man he could continue to live with the child. But in a prison cell . . .

He dismissed these thoughts. He had to stay focused and alert, and to stop thinking about the terrible things that broke his heart and weakened his legs.

As the morning went on, the flow of farmers and buyers grew in the adjacent streets. Trucks with muddy wheels parked near the market, unloading their cargo of bleating and bellowing cattle, while men in ponchos shouted and blew on piercing whistles. In the midst of this human and animal commotion, Angel and Paolo welcomed the protection that the crowd offered them, so they let themselves be pushed from right to left and left to right, following the flux.

When they arrived near the boxes, Angel noticed a man in uniform. He quickly turned back and dragged Paolo along to the shelter of a house porch.

"Go and look," he said. "Be careful."

Paolo made his way toward the boxes. Posters of Angel were glued on wooden posts. Three policemen were keeping watch over the donkey and horse. The child recognized the farmer from the Pampas, whose horse they had stolen; he was kicking his heels in front of the boxes. The Belgian alpinist was not there. Maybe he was still shouting at the top of his lungs out on the desolate plain, or maybe his embassy had sent him back to his mountainless country. . . .

As fluid as a snake, Paolo left and returned to the porch where Angel was waiting. They no longer had any means of transportation, or money, or place to hide in town. Paolo observed Angel's face, his tense features, the cold glimmer in his eyes.

"As long as they're looking for me at the market, we have a chance," Angel said.

Paolo took his hand. "I'll do what you want," he said. "But don't leave me."

Angel gave Paolo's hand a gentle squeeze and swore that he would never abandon him. Paolo was the only person in the world to whom he could make promises, the only one to whom he could say words as improbable as *always* and *never*. He pulled Paolo onto the crowded street and headed toward the harbor.

On this festive day, the whole town was in a frenzy. Cars blocked the main roads, horses and pedestrians crowded the sidewalks, and, near the harbor, the cries of the seagulls competed with the honking cars.

Several trawlers had just docked. It was time to unload the cases. Paolo and Angel did not stay there long. They crossed the congested piers, keeping as low a profile as possible, until they finally reached the marina. There, at the very end, Angel saw what he was looking for.

"Do you see that large red ship?" he asked Paolo.

"Yes."

"We're in luck."

"Are we going aboard?"

"No, they check the passenger list."

Without trying to understand, Paolo continued to trot alongside Angel, who was taking long strides as he headed toward the ship. The child could see the red cuirass of the boat against the white cliff behind it. *B-o-t-e.* Luis had forgotten to tell him how to spell this word correctly and he thought he might never find out. Why was it that people did not finish what they started? Only Angel, it seemed to him, was able to finish the task he set his mind on: killing someone was a way to finish things. And right now he could feel the power of the murderer, his determination and obstinance. Paolo trusted him: if Angel had promised not to abandon him *ever,* he would keep his word. And maybe he would even manage to buy the lamb, though with the posters of Angel plastered over every fence in the cattle market, it was unlikely.

Close to the red ship were travelers, piles of bags, stacks of heavy trunks, as well as employees of the shipping line, who were checking tickets.

"Wait for me here," Angel said. "Don't move."

Paolo stayed near the trunks. He couldn't see what Angel was up to, and his heart beat madly.

Angel rushed toward the line of passengers. Just as he had thought, Delia and Luis were there. From the moment he had seen them at the bank, Angel had grasped their plan.

Their backs were turned to him. They looked like newlyweds going off on their honeymoon. Angel's hand went under his vest. The knife was in the same spot in his pocket. He placed the blade directly between Luis's shoulder blades, stinging him.

"Not a word," Angel whispered in Luis's ear. "Come with me. And Delia too, or else I'll kill you."

Quick, discreet, that was Angel's way. He was used to the reaction of his victims. Their bodies went limp and they broke into a sweat; then he could do whatever he wanted with them.

Delia and Luis left the passenger line. Angel pushed them toward the big metallic trunks, where Paolo was waiting quietly. There Angel pushed a little more on the knife handle until Luis's face contorted in pain. With his other hand, the murderer held the back of Delia's neck, his fingers clenched in her thick hair.

"Why don't you tell Paolo?" Angel said. "He'll be very surprised to learn what you were about to do."

Paolo looked at Luis and did not need words to understand.

"Are you going around the world with Delia?" he asked, just for confirmation.

Breathless and shaking, Luis could do nothing but nod.

"But . . . the weird vegetables?" Paolo said. "And the water that makes you sick? And the heat that gives you headaches?"

"There comes a time when you have to confront your fears," Luis answered, his eyes filled with sorrow.

He could not explain to this young and naive child that he had at last gathered the strength to pull away from his own childhood, and that he could never become a man unless he went away now. That was the way it was: cruel and necessary.

Paolo turned to Delia. He wanted to know how she had managed to convince Luis to go. But he didn't ask her, guessing that there must be secrets only adults knew.

Angel pushed on the knife handle again, and the blade went through Luis's shirt. Luis winced.

"You forgot to give Paolo money to buy the sheep," Angel went on. "That's not nice."

"The sheep and the lamb," Paolo specified.

Delia had started to cry. Angel shook her.

"You draw nice portraits," he blurted out. "But I prefer your landscapes."

"Don't kill us!" Delia begged.

"If Luis gives me half of his money, I'll let you board the ship."

Angel had said all he had to say. No negotiation was possible. Luis collapsed a little more. In addition to fear, he could feel shame knotting his stomach. Paolo's eyes, honest and full of hope, hurt him much more than the knife between his shoulder blades. Angel gave him time to recover and open his bag. Inside was a huge pile of bills. Luis's whole inheritance. He took half of it out and gave it to Paolo without uttering a word.

"Thank you," Paolo said.

At that very moment, the horn of the big red ship blew. Boarding time was coming to an end.

"Hurry!" Angel said as he put his knife back in his pocket. "You wouldn't want to miss your trip around the world!"

Luis picked up his belongings. Delia took his arm. And together they ran to the gangway. Paolo saw them climb over it, then disappear into the belly of the boat. In his small hand, the bills were shaking like the leaves of a willow.

CHAPTER EIGHTEEN

IT'S NOT EASY *to be alive,* Paolo was thinking as he walked alongside Angel. *It's complicated, twisted and kinked, just like the dead trees of the Pampas.*

He touched the yellow sweet in his pocket with the tips of his fingers. He believed that the talisman had brought him luck, since he and Angel were leaving Punta Arenas free and rich. But, at the same time, he doubted its power. Happiness wasn't fleeing town in the dark of a cold night, or balancing on the edge of a crumbling cliff where one could tumble at any moment. If it existed, happiness more likely resembled the plush carpeting at the bank, the comfort of heat, and the lamb with its dense fleece. It was a father, a mother who knew how to hug her child, friends who didn't leave to travel around the world, women who were content to paint fishing villages and who didn't give sketches to the police. . . .

But, for now, Paolo had to be satisfied with what he had: the stolen banknotes and Angel. Angel with his knife.

"I'm hungry," Paolo said.

"So am I."

"My legs hurt."

"Do you want me to carry you?"

"You won't be able to for long. I'm heavy."

"To me, you're light."

Angel stopped, lifted Paolo over his head, and sat him on his shoulders. It was a clear night. A huge moon was following them, providing light. At the bottom of the cliff, the waves were crashing without respite. A long while ago they had passed the spot where Paolo had wanted to jump.

"I wonder if the alpinist is dead," Paolo said.

Angel smiled a smile that Paolo did not see but that he heard. Very little time had elapsed since their encounter with the Belgian man, and yet they had the impression of talking about a very distant moment, a moment as old as the Flood.

"Luis and Delia—" Paolo started to say.

"Leave those two where they belong. We'll never see them again, and that's for the best."

Angel was focusing on the stones and potholes along the path. On his shoulders, the child was slowly swaying; they looked like a two-headed animal.

"Have you already been in love?" Paolo asked suddenly.

"I believe so. . . . I don't know."

"Does it hurt?"

"Not at the beginning, but after, it does."

"Can it hurt other people?"

Angel sighed deeply. He did not mind walking all night long with the load on his shoulders, but he had to think hard about the child's serious questions before he could give any answers.

"Are you asking because Luis hurt you?" he inquired.

"A little."

"He betrayed us," Angel declared.

"And you, will you betray me too?"

"Never, Paolo. Never."

Paolo kept to himself the many other questions that were troubling him. He guessed that he would have to live a long time before finding the answers.

They went on silently. After a while, Angel noticed that Paolo was drifting to sleep and was about to topple. There was no shelter: only the path, the stones, the cliff, and the heath. It was hard to believe that with all their money, they could not afford a little rest and some heat!

Angel brought the child down and took him in his arms. Paolo's head nestled against the crook of Angel's shoulder. His body went limp and he fell asleep.

All night Angel walked, his eyes protruding and muscles stiffening from the effort. At dawn, he reached the ruins of a sheep pen. He went in, put Paolo down on a heap of straw, and sighed in relief.

When they woke up, the sun was already high in the sky. The wind had subsided, the weather was mild. Without uttering a word, the man and the child started to walk again, leaving the shore and the cliffs behind to go deeper inland, each of them preoccupied by somber thoughts.

After two hours, they caught sight of the first trees of a forest in the northeast and, far behind it, of the jagged mountaintops hanging in the sky above the clouds. A feeling of death, rather than life, emanated from this forest, whose trees were bent and ruffled by the violent winds.

Angel walked in front, telling Paolo when to lift his feet high to avoid tripping on the roots and branches that had fallen to the ground. At the same time, Angel listened for noises and kept an eye out for a rodent, a mole, any small animal that could be hunted as game. But life was not taking hold in the sparse, dry undergrowth.

Yet as they went deeper into the forest, they noticed some changes. On the ground, moss was replaced by short ferns, then by taller and larger ones. They looked up and saw that the canopy of trees was becoming thicker, trapping the humidity under its uneven cover. The light was also dipping because they were reaching the buttress of the mountains.

To pluck up his courage, Paolo hurried to catch up with

Angel and put his small hand in the murderer's. Straight ahead the forest looked forebodingly dark. The child remembered what Luis had told him about confronting fears. Paolo thought that if he came out of the forest alive, maybe then he would be a man.

"Do you hear that?" Angel whispered suddenly.

Paolo became attentive. "Yes."

Different faraway sounds reached their ears: the echo of an ax splitting wood; the humming of an engine; then silence, followed again by the hacking of wood. Somewhere deep in the forest, a lumberjack was working, and these human sounds reassured Paolo. He followed Angel, his face grazed by the ferns, his eyes wide open in the half-light. A few birds could be seen high in the trees. He could hardly see the sky any longer.

They reached the spot where the lumberjack had been working. A tree that had been recently felled lay across the way. They saw the ax, the chain saw, and a coat that hung on a low branch, as well as a bottle of water and some provisions, which they looked at with hunger but did not touch. The lumberjack was nowhere in sight.

"What do we do?" Paolo asked.

"We sit down," Angel suggested.

They sat on a stump, pressed against each other. Paolo was so tired that even his fear had diminished. He lay down across Angel's knees, his eyes turned upward to the canopy of trees. It seemed to him then that there was no better hiding place in the world than this one. The Punta Arenas police, the farmer, the alpinist, no one could hunt them out here. It was like being at the bottom of a deep hole. He could feel Angel's warmth under his back, and under his legs the thickness of the wood, which connected him to some powerful and indestructible force deep in the ground. And so he fell asleep and dreamed he was a tree.

Angel heard a rustle of leaves. He did not move a muscle. It was the lumberjack. He emerged from the ferns and nearly screamed, but Angel put a finger across his lips to signal that a child was sleeping. The man looked surprised, but came closer. He was an old man, his skin tanned and wrinkled. His beard was like a frozen lake around his mouth, and his eyes were as blue as forget-me-nots. He was a summary of the seasons here, winter and summer intermingled.

"We walked a long time," Angel told him softly.

"Would you like some water?" the man asked. He went to fetch his bottle and handed it to Angel. "My name is Ricardo Murga. Do you have shelter for the night?"

Angel shook his head, but he already knew that this man would take them in. And he knew he would not have to kill him.

CHAPTER NINETEEN

RICARDO MURGA WAS seventy-five years old and lived alone on the north edge of the forest. He had built his house himself when his wife was expecting their first child, more than fifty years before. A lumberjack and carpenter by trade, he had chosen this isolated spot where he could work without ever having to go too far from his family.

"We had three children: two sons and a daughter. Each time a child was born, I added a room to the house. Now they are no longer here. You'll see, there is plenty of space for you."

It was twilight when they got out of the forest. Paolo followed the two men absentmindedly. He was so hungry that his stomach hurt, and he could taste the acidity of his saliva.

Ricardo opened the door to his home. He stepped back to let his guests enter. The warmth and comfort of the house were surprising: rugs, velvet-covered armchairs, a couch with a small stand on each side, windows with curtains, knickknacks . . . and, even more unexpected, a huge library where books crowded the shelves. It was not at all what anyone would have thought the house of an old, lonely lumberjack would look like.

Ricardo lit two oil lamps as well as a multitude of small candles, which he put on the table.

"My wife was from Holland," he said with a smile. "The interior of the house is hers. By lighting the candles, I feel I'm perpetuating her memory."

He disappeared into a room and brought back a loaf of bread and glasses, as well as a dish containing a leftover leg of lamb. This was going to be a real feast! Paolo attacked the food without saying a word. His cheeks took on some color, his eyes glistened again like fresh chestnuts, and his whole body shook with pleasure.

Seated in an armchair, Ricardo observed his guests silently and with curiosity. He had learned to keep quiet and to accept the surprises that life brought him. A man and an exhausted child had appeared in the forest. Well, they must have had their reasons to wander this far.

"I would like to drink some wine with you," he said to

Angel. "I've a few rare bottles that I don't allow myself to open when I'm alone."

As he got up, Paolo smiled and said a heartfelt "Thank you," but not before a big burp escaped from his lips. Ricardo bowed slightly and tried to hide his amusement by closing the door behind him.

"You should have restrained yourself," Angel whispered. "We're not among savages here!"

Angel was very impressed by the old man and his simple and comfortable surroundings. His hospitality deeply baffled the murderer, who for the first time in a long while did not feel any animosity against one of his fellow men.

Paolo did not care about being reprimanded. He curled himself like a cat on the cushions of the sofa; he could feel the sweet in his pocket when he brought his knees up to his chin. Once more, the talisman had worked: how else to explain their encounter with such a good man?

Ricardo came back and poured a very dark wine into the glasses.

"I bought this bottle years ago from a Valparaiso wine merchant," he said.

"We know someone who lived in Valparaiso too!" Paolo said.

Ricardo smiled and lifted his glass. In the trembling light of the candles, the wine took on a deep and silky purple color.

"Then let's drink to Valparaiso."

"To Valparaiso," Angel repeated.

More drinks, more words...Little by little Paolo became sleepy. He had the feeling he was in a boat, on a nasty sea; but that nothing bad could happen to him while on board.

Ricardo explained to Angel that the felled tree in the forest was the very last one he would chop down before his definite retirement. The next day he would cut it up and bring it back piece by piece.

"I sell my wood to merchants. They come with their trucks, load it, and then go. This is the last order I will accept."

"To your last order," Angel said, lifting his glass.

"And to lumber!" Ricardo added. "I have lived all my life thanks to lumber. I have fed myself. I have taken shelter from the rain. I have heated the house. And I have read nearly all my books, which are made from wood fibers."

Ricardo's voice was warm and appeasing. He spoke softly, like someone who has nothing to prove, and yet each of his words seemed to hide a secret.

"I like metamorphosis," he said. He sighed and swirled the wine in his glass. "Wood that becomes books. Winter that becomes spring. Grapes that become wine." He turned to Paolo. "And the child who becomes a man."

Paolo, at the edge of sleepiness, smiled. "It's true, I went through the forest. I'm no longer afraid," he said.

"Some changes are very subtle," the lumberjack went on. "Those which happen in our soul, for example, are not always noticeable."

Angel moved in his chair, suddenly feeling uneasy.

"Do you mean . . . ," he began, intimidated; "do you mean that men can change their nature?"

"I believe so," Ricardo answered. "And you?"

"I don't know," Angel whispered.

Ricardo got up and opened a drawer at the bottom of his bookshelves. He took out a tiny box and pushed the cover open with his thumb. The box contained tobacco, which he silently rolled into a cigarette.

"The forest produces millions of plant species," he said, leaning toward the flame of a candle. "We know almost nothing of the forest."

He took a puff of the cigarette and blew a very fragrant bluish smoke through his nose.

"I transformed one of these plants into a special tobacco. It is one achievable metamorphosis. One of the mysteries surrounding us."

He offered a smoke to Angel. Silence descended on the house. Paolo was slowly drifting to sleep, among the blue exhalations of the strange plant.

"Poets also know how to transform things," Ricardo Murga added. "They look at the world and they absorb it like a drink. And then when they start talking, nothing is the same. It is like magic. Each day I try to look at the world with such eyes. This is what keeps me going."

"I can read too," Paolo muttered in his half-sleep.

"I'll lend you my books," Ricardo promised.

Under his heavy eyelids, Paolo wondered about the books piled up on the shelves. There were so many! Would an entire lifetime be enough to decipher those millions of words? He could not believe that this man, even as old as he was, had read almost all of them. Unless he was a magician, which, of course, was quite possible.

CHAPTER TWENTY

THE WINE FROM the Valparaiso merchant, the blue tobacco, the exhaustion from the long walks these last days, and the very Dutch comfort of the bed had their effect: Angel slept like a log. He woke up with the impression of being born anew, his head heavy on the softness of the feather pillow, his limbs relaxed, and for a while he listened to the calm rhythm of his heart. He had not felt so young and full of strength in years.

Ricardo had put him in his elder son's bedroom. His daughter's, next door, had gone to Paolo. After falling asleep on the couch, the child had not even noticed when Angel tucked him into a bed with white sheets so clean, so delicately perfumed, that they seemed intended for a prince.

Angel stretched. Daylight was dancing in the folds of the curtains, and he thought he could hear people talking outside. He got up, put his clothes on, and left the room. The whole house smelled of warm bread and coffee. Did he, a murderer, a thief, deserve to spend even one more moment in this enchanted place? Was he not going to sully its purity? While walking through the house, Angel tried to make himself inconspicuous and as light as air.

Then he stopped in the open doorway, stupefied.

Dancing on the grass wet with sparkling dew, Paolo was roaring with laughter in the company of three children his own age.

Farther away, next to the woodshed, Ricardo was standing in the sun, his hands in his pockets. Bewildered, Angel approached the round of dancing children. Who were they? Where had they come from? What means of transp—

"Don't disturb them," Ricardo said, putting his hand on Angel's arm. "They're having such a good time!"

Angel's eyes were riveted to the man's pupils as he tried to find answers to his questions.

"Come," Ricardo suggested. "Breakfast is waiting for you inside."

Angel followed him back into the house while the children erupted in laughter.

On the low table near the couch, Ricardo poured coffee into glistening china cups and held one out to Angel.

"Don't try to understand," Ricardo advised. "If there is one thing that life has taught me, it's to accept even the most foolish and unthinkable happiness. Welcome this happiness and don't speak. All the questions you're asking yourself are useless. You saw them—the three of them—as well as I did, didn't you? And just as well as your son, who held their hands as they all danced."

Angel swallowed a gulp of coffee. He wanted to protest, to shout that it was not possible, that the dead are dead! But he said nothing.

"For forty years, each morning, my heart fills with joy. Do you understand, sir?" Ricardo asked.

Angel shook his head.

"Just before I leave to go into the forest to fell trees, they come to say hello and play under my windows, like in old times. Without their visits, I would not have had the courage to go on. Or to work. Or to live. Sometimes at night, my wife also comes back. It seems to me that her visits coincide with the harvest of the blue tobacco. I see her come in, her cotton cap on her head. It's an extraordinary moment."

Ricardo handed Angel a silver basket in which he had arranged slices of toasted bread. Angel took one delicately between his fingers.

"Joana was only eight years old," Ricardo went on. "Dimitri had just celebrated his tenth birthday, and Sven, the eldest, whose bedroom you used last night, was going to be thirteen. One day long ago, they went north with their mother. There was to be a feast at the farm of family members to celebrate the last day of harvest, when the wheat is threshed. I had to finish a job in the forest and was going to join them later on. When they left—I remember it so well!—they were blowing kisses at me, and my wife was cracking the whip above the head of the mare hitched to the cart. 'See you soon, Papa! Try to come quickly!' the children yelled."

He caught his breath, and Angel, who sat motionless on the sofa, noticed tears drowning the old lumberjack's blue eyes.

"They never reached the farm where the party was to be held. What happened? I don't really know. They probably came across someone on their way. This person, whose name I'll never know, robbed them. And then killed them. The four of them. Like that. I'm the one who discovered them, the next day, on my way to the harvest fest, as I was spurring my horse to speed up."

Silence fell again. Angel was shaking. The coffee in his china cup was about to spill. With effort, he put it down on the table.

"Now, if you will excuse me," Ricardo whispered, getting up.

He went to the door. On his way out, he removed his hat from the stand and put it on his head. "I have to take care of my last order," he said.

Angel remained immobile for a long while, his head ringing with the most violent, most painful, and strangest thoughts one would expect from a murderer. Then he too got up and went out.

Ricardo's children had gone. They had left when their father had started his tractor, and Paolo was now killing time by dragging his feet in the dust. Angel approached him very slowly. He wondered if Paolo was going to disappear too. Was he going to evaporate before Angel's eyes? Was he somehow going to be a victim of the mysterious powers of this place? At that instant, Angel fully appreciated the meaning of the word *bewitching*.

"My friends went home," Paolo complained when he saw Angel. "It's unfair! Why didn't they stay with me? I was having a lot of fun."

Angel crouched and sat the child on his knees. He could feel Paolo's skin, warm and damp with perspiration, and the roundness of his arms. The child was a tangible reality, and yes, Paolo seemed less skinny than before.

"Your friends will come back tomorrow morning," he whispered.

"Are you sure?"

"Sure!"

Paolo smiled. "So does that mean that we're going to stay a little longer at Ricardo's?"

"A little. I believe he needs us today."

"In the forest?"

"Yes. We should help him cut his last tree and bring it here. Don't you agree?"

Cheered up, Paolo jumped from Angel's knees. He ran into the house and came back with a large slice of bread and jam.

"I have to build up strength to cut wood," he said very seriously.

Together they set out into the forest, the child skipping joyously in front, the man walking behind, prey to an inner anguish that was extracting secret tears from him.

CHAPTER TWENTY-ONE

ANGEL GAVE ALL his strength, all his energy, all his
fervor to Ricardo's last order. He spent the whole day running along the felled tree, cutting the biggest limbs with the
chain saw, and chopping the smaller ones with the ax. He
bounced around, pulling, tearing, knocking; he was perspiring and exhausting himself; he was smiling.

Ricardo came and sat down on the stump next to
Paolo.

"What debt do you think your father wants to repay?"
the old lumberjack asked, amused.

Paolo, who was watching Angel strive so hard, and who

was waiting for someone to give him permission to bundle the twigs, answered what was evident to him.

"He would like to undo the harm he has done."

"I don't think Angel could have done any harm," Ricardo answered.

"Oh, he has," Paolo said.

He turned toward the lumberjack and smiled. He was delighted that he could surprise a man as old and as well-read as this one.

"Angel has killed people," he said. "But don't tell him that you know. He would be angry with me."

Confused, Ricardo gave his promise, not entirely sure of what he had just heard. Was the child joking? Was he crazy? Or, if what he said was true, could the ax and the chain saw become dangerous tools?

No, really, Ricardo could not believe that Angel was a murderer. Since the death of his family, he thought he had developed an extra sense that enabled him to detect the presence of evil. He thought he could guess the bad intentions of any passerby at first sight. This was how he had chased away a few peddlers from the limits of his property, and some merchants with treacherous eyes, just because of the way they walked or rode their horses. So if he had given shelter to a murderer, he would know it!

Nevertheless, he got up and went back prudently toward the tree. Angel, astride the trunk, was beginning to cut it up. Sheaves of sawdust rose around him like frightened bee swarms. Sensing Ricardo's presence, he stopped working and cut the motor of the chain saw.

"You must be worn out," Ricardo said. "Come and drink some water and have a bite to eat."

Angel shook his head. "No, thanks," he said, taking off the goggles that Ricardo had lent him.

"It's going to be a long day."

"Workdays go faster than one thinks," Angel declared.

"You're clever," Ricardo went on. "You must have done this kind of work before. Am I wrong?"

"I've done a little bit of everything."

"And the child? He follows you like that, from place to place?"

"Yes. He has nobody else."

As a rule, Ricardo never asked personal questions, and one of his principles was to respect the privacy of others. But this time, he felt a tremendous desire to know everything about this man and child. Questions were crowding his lips, burning his tongue. But Angel put his goggles back on and started the chain saw. That cut the conversation short.

The day went on like this, in the changing shade of the undergrowth and over the clamor of the chain saw. Paolo trotted around the large broken trunk, collecting twigs, carrying full loads of them near the stump, and then sorted them according to size before bundling them up.

"You'll have a good supply for your fireplace," he said to Ricardo, proudly showing the bundles.

The old woodcutter smiled. "If I survive the winter!"

"Are you that old?"

"I don't have many more books to read," he answered.

With wonder, the child imagined Ricardo's books as a supply of oxygen. If a life span was so tightly linked to the number of books one possessed, then this helped to explain the sudden death of his parents. In their home, there had not been one single book! Paolo promised himself to buy a lot of them with his money.

"Where do you buy books?" he asked.

"In town. In bookstores. Sometimes the peddlers have one or two, but they are not very good."

"I would like to go to a bookstore. Do you think there's one in Puerto Natales?"

"Are you going that way?"

"No, but I could buy a horse to go there. I have a lot of money now that Luis gave me half of his inheritance."

"Luis?"

"He's a friend. Well, he was. He's gone to travel around the world because he's in love."

Ricardo nodded. "That's right, love can take you far away!"

He thought about his wife. He had met her in Holland, when he was a student there. At the time he dreamed of living like a European, far from the wilds of Chile, in towns with paved roads, in tall, clean houses, like those he had seen in Vermeer's paintings. But after a while, he had grown homesick and his wife had followed him here because she loved him.

"Do you think there's a bookstore in Puerto Natales?" Paolo asked again.

"Probably."

Paolo was piling up his bundles joyously. The future seemed radiant: He and Angel were going to spend a few more nights at Ricardo's, and he would be able to play again with the children in the wet grass. Then he and Angel would go north. They would go back home, to the lonely house, and once well rested, they would go up to Puerto Natales. After all, not having a lamb was not so terrible. Instead, Paolo would have the books. And, if Paolo asked him, Angel would build bookshelves that they could prop up with stones against the crooked wall of the house. How pleasant it would be! He forgot all about the problems at Punta Arenas: Delia's deceitful hugs, Luis's betrayal, the red ship, Angel's knife—even his desire to die at the edge of the cliff. From now on, he was going to live a different life, a beautiful and comfortable life.

At twilight, Angel and Ricardo loaded the lumber onto the trailer behind the tractor. Only a few heaps of sawdust, a clean stump, and some wood chips, where the tree had broken some branches of neighboring pines when falling, were left on the ground. Paolo sighed with pleasure and looked up at the pinkish sky between the mountaintops. He felt tired, as well as grateful toward the two men. Thanks to them, he would never again be afraid to enter a forest. He was glad to have conquered his fear. One small victory after another, wasn't that the way to grow up?

"What will happen to your tree?" he asked Ricardo.

"Someone will pick it up tonight. Someone from the sawmill."

"And then?"

"Then it will be cut up. It will provide dozens of nice planks for carpentry or cabinetmaking."

Paolo smiled. "It'll be metamorphosed!" he concluded cheerfully.

He contemplated the large, freshly cut round logs. Drops of resin were forming at their ends, little ocher or brown stalactites that looked like tears. Ricardo started the tractor. It was the last time he would be bringing a load home. He wished he could bestow a solemn touch on this final trip by driving slowly enough to enjoy every spot of soil, each centimeter of the road, but he feared that it would awaken his melancholy. So, instead, he recited the verses of a poem.

> "My heart goes on cutting wood,
> singing with the sawmills in the rain,
> milling together cold, sawdust, wood smell."

Paolo was seated on the hood at the front of the tractor. With each jolt along the path, he laughed. Behind him, Angel and Ricardo were silent, like all men who are exhausted and satisfied with their work. The fatigue had pushed the questions back. Ricardo no longer felt their fire on his tongue. Whoever this man next to him was, and whatever he had done in his life, he had proved his honesty and his courage here, on the trunk of the tree. That was enough, and Ricardo felt at peace.

When they were close enough to see the house, they saw a truck parked in the yard. A large blond man in blue overalls got out.

"Hello!" he shouted.

Ricardo waved to him, while Angel lowered his head to hide his face.

When they reached the man, Ricardo stopped the tractor.

"The sawmill sent me," the man explained.

"Couldn't Alfredo come himself?" Ricardo asked.

"This timber has to be taken to Puerto Natales without delay," the man answered. "It's not going to be treated at the usual sawmill. Do you want to see the order slip?"

Ricardo went with the man to the truck; Angel took advantage of this to jump out of the tractor. He grabbed Paolo in his arms.

"Come, let them take care of business."

He took the child to the shelter of the house. Obviously, Ricardo had been expecting someone else; Angel was suspicious; surprises were seldom good news for murderers. He stood near the window, behind the half-drawn curtains, to observe the blond giant. He saw Ricardo look at the papers, sign at the bottom of a sheet, then help the man remove the straps holding the timber to the trailer.

Paolo asked whether he could go out to watch the

action, but Angel stopped him with a commanding look. The child noticed Angel's hands touching his chest nervously, moving like insects around a bright light. He knew what it meant.

Paolo shrugged and went to curl up on the soft couch. After a while, the truck left; he could hear it going down the path, carrying the last tree, along with Angel's suspicions.

Ricardo looked worried when he came back to the house. He was holding the order slip in his hand. But when he saw the child nestled on the couch, and Angel standing near the window, he smiled and left the piece of paper on the corner of a table. He realized how fast he had become attached to his guests. Especially to Paolo.

"Thank you," he said, "for helping me with my work. Tonight we will drink to bygone days and to my retirement."

He noticed that Angel was looking at the slip of paper.

"Don't worry," Ricardo added, "everything is in order. I'm just getting old and things are changing. The sawmill of my friend Alfredo subcontracts part of its orders. You see, I'm glad I'm retiring. Before, Alfredo would come himself and we would have a drink and talk for a while before settling our business. But this man did not inspire me, so I did not invite him in."

"You did the right thing," Angel said.

"Did he take your tree to Puerto Natales?" Paolo asked.

"Well, yes. I'm told it's a special order for a town institution. But I couldn't care less about it now." Ricardo removed his hat and his leather jacket, then turned to Angel. "You can stay as long as you want. You're not disturbing me."

"Tomorrow, we shall go home," Angel answered.

"What is calling you to your house? Are there animals to tend to?"

"No," said Paolo. "Our goats are dead. They were old. My fox too is dead. And my par—"

"We have things to do," Angel interrupted. "That's all."

Paolo was sad. He wanted to stay longer in this house on the outskirts of the forest, and he noticed that Ricardo looked sorry as well. But Paolo did not want to upset Angel by asking the reasons for his decision.

Silently they dined on a piece of deer that Ricardo had kept for a special occasion. In the trembling light of the candles, their eyes seemed animated by a strange and autonomous life, as if the agitation of their souls were reflected in their pupils.

"It's a very special day," Ricardo said. He put his fork down. "If you leave tomorrow, I would like . . ."

He got up, his face as pink as a summer dawn. He motioned to Paolo and Angel to wait for him, then disappeared into a nearby room.

"When we're gone, he'll be all alone," Paolo whispered. "Do you think he's going to die?"

Angel wiped his mouth with the corner of his cotton napkin. Death, he knew death so well. But he knew only its violence, its way of cutting short the lives of people still very young, due to illness or the blade of his knife. He had never seen anyone die peacefully, slowly, as if going to sleep.

"We can come back one day," he said to Paolo. "Ricardo will be waiting for us."

A moment later, the old lumberjack walked in, carrying a large box in his arms. Without a word, he put it down on one of the side tables and opened it. Paolo wondered what new treasure he was going to discover. Once the cover had been lifted, he could see a strange apparatus.

"I hope it still works," Ricardo muttered. "It belonged to my wife, and I have not used it in years."

He removed a large, black, shiny disk from its jacket and laid it flat on the machine. Then he cranked a handle on the side of the box.

Angel's eyes shrank. He stared intensely at Paolo. And when Ricardo moved the arm of the old phonograph, he held his breath. He guessed that Paolo had never heard music, not even the sound of a flute made from a reed, or even that of a rattle. The child only knew the violent howling of the wind pushing at the sides of the house down on the desolate heath.

The record gave out some crackling and static sounds. Ricardo stood up, a finger on his lips, his eyes half closed.

The sound of violins invaded the room, together with that of cellos. It was an elongated sound, reinforced by the slow pulsations of an organ.

Paolo did not budge.

The modulation of the strings undulated, going higher, coming lower, swirling, darting and crisscrossing, while the organ kept the somber and slow pace of a funeral march. This music seemed sad and full of hope all at once. Earthly and heavenly, heavy and light; it was summing up all that Paolo had understood from life these past few days.

He was shaking in his seat; his eyes blurred.

In the music, he recognized the softness of the fox, the warmth of the lamb, but also Luis's betrayal, and all the stones and pebbles that had made him trip along his journey. He did not see Angel, or Ricardo, or the polished furniture, or the candles. Memories burst before him as if each note were a hook fishing out the feelings buried in his soul. As if he had become an ocean, a river.

Angel saw the tears running down Paolo's cheeks. He saw the old man standing near his phonograph, absorbing the beauty of the music.

The murderer put his large hands flat on his knees, as he too fell victim to the spell of the organ, the violins, the solemn rhythm, and the clear, harmonious sounds that seemed to want to pull his heart up to heaven. It *was* beautiful, so different from what he had known in his life so far. A sigh lifted his chest.

For a long while they remained silent, letting the music unfurl and embrace them. The warmth of the house felt good. An immense peace filled their hearts, lulling all suf-

fering. Angel wished he could live this way forever, surrounded by beauty and calm, far from the world, the cities,
the pubs and their crude lights, the shouts and the crowds.
Why was he discovering this happiness only now?

Suddenly a terrible anxiety clutched his throat. He realized that the music had come too late for him. It would
never alleviate the enormity and foolishness of his crimes.

But what about Paolo?

He looked at the child, at his confused little face, his
delicate hands. For Paolo, it was not too late! And he,
Angel, did not have the right to deprive him of all this. He
had taken the child away from his solitude; now he had to
set him free.

Angel suppressed a sob. In a few seconds, his decision
was made: he was going to entrust Paolo to Ricardo. If he
accomplished only one act of love in this world, it had to be
now. He would give Paolo the possibility of a better life.
That would be his act of love.

When the music stopped, Ricardo put the record back
in its jacket, then pulled the cover of the box down.

Paolo had not moved from his chair. He looked like a
statue. Angel was suffocating. The more the silence lin-
gered, the more the idea of separation took hold in his
mind. Paolo would stay with the old man, with the books
on the shelves, the phonograph and its music, and the mysteries of the forest.

Yes, he was going to give Paolo to Ricardo, and Ricardo

to Paolo. Together they would find a meaning to life, whereas he, a killer, would continue to wander alone on the rough roads ahead, with remorse his only company.

He wanted to express what was in his heart, but Paolo rose suddenly and approached Ricardo.

"What was it?" Paolo whispered.

The old man smiled, crouched in front of him, and handed him the record. Paolo bent his head. There were letters on the jacket.

"Jo . . . Johann . . . Sebastian . . . Bach," he deciphered.

"It's the name of the man who composed this piece," Ricardo explained. "If you like it, keep it, it's yours."

Paolo opened his mouth but did not say anything. He squeezed the record against his chest and, overwhelmed with gratitude, kissed Ricardo's wrinkled cheek.

Angel was thunderstruck. Paolo had never kissed him, had never shown as much tenderness toward him. Everything was definitely decided now. He had to act right away.

Angel took out the knife hidden in his pocket and fingered the patina of the handle, a patina acquired during brawls and potato-peeling chores. He approached Paolo.

Ricardo gave a start when he saw the shining blade. He grabbed Paolo, pulling him back quickly.

"Watch out!" he shouted.

Angel froze in front of them. He was so tall that he towered above the old man and the small child. They were at his mercy—two fragile beings whose fate was in his hands. He looked at Paolo.

"Take it," he said, "it's for you."

The silence was complete. The reflection of the candle-light danced on the blade of the knife. Ricardo trembled as he held the child against him.

"Take it," Angel said again, his voice breaking.

Slowly Paolo let go of the record with one hand and let the knife fall into it.

"Do whatever you want with it," Angel whispered. "You can throw it to the bottom of a well or leave it forever in a drawer. I'm going to bed now."

He left the room.

Paolo remained motionless, his fingers gripping the record and the knife so hard that they hurt. His torn heart was bleeding in his chest and he wondered why things had to be so. Why did he always have to make a choice: between Angel and Ricardo, music and Angel, love and poetry, words and actions, leaving and staying, life and dreams, dreams and Angel, when all he hoped for was to bring all of them together?

"Then it's true," Ricardo said after a while. "Angel did kill people?"

Paolo nodded. But he knew that it was over now, that Angel would never hurt anyone again. The knife was heavy in his hand.

✥

That night, Ricardo realized he had made a mistake. His discerning mind had lost its acuity with age and he had not been able to discern the true nature of Angel Allegria. But the truth had been revealed: there was a dangerous man under his roof who, even without his knife, remained a murderer. Before going to bed, he went to fetch his old hunting rifle to keep it with him in his room.

✧

Very late that night, Angel left the sleepy house. He had lain on the bed of Ricardo's dead son for a long time, his eyes open, before making his decision. When he opened the front door and felt the coolness of the night on his face, he knew he was making the right choice. He had to disappear from Paolo's life.

He tiptoed across the grass of the yard, passed by the empty woodshed, then took the path to the north. It was the same route Ricardo's wife and children had taken to go to the harvest fest, and he had a strange feeling that he was going to meet them along the way. He was walking to a secret meeting with ghosts.

CHAPTER TWENTY-TWO

THE POLICE OF Punta Arenas made use of all the means at their disposal. Delia's sketch had been circulated on the national police network, and, because of it, Angel Allegria had been identified as a dangerous criminal. He was already wanted in Talcahuano, Temuco, and Puerto Natales. Wasting no time, the commissioner put his most qualified men and their teams on his trail.

Delia's father had given a deposition that stated that not only was Angel Allegria a criminal, but he had also kidnapped a child, whom he was abusing. Delia's father went on to mention Luis Secundo, describing him as an upstanding citizen of Valparaiso who had been forced to give Angel money. Fortunately, Delia had managed to rescue Luis from the hands of this monster; Mr. Secunda was now free and safe.

The horse merchants were interrogated: none of them had sold any animals to the murderer.

Identity checks were conducted at the harbor, the airport, and the railroad station; squads of armed law enforcement officers were sent to inns and pubs. Traffic slowed considerably around the town where roadblocks had been placed.

After three days of intense but fruitless searching, the commissioner decided to extend the perimeter of his combing. It seemed likely that the man had gone north, so two motorized teams and their tracking dogs—dogs that had sniffed the bedsheets on which Angel had slept at the inn— were sent on the road. The manhunt had begun.

CHAPTER TWENTY-THREE

PAOLO WOKE UP with a red mark on his left cheek because he had fallen asleep on the record. As for the knife, he had put it under the belt of his pants, thinking it might be useful: he could always cut twigs to make small toys.

In anticipation of this new day, he went out, hoping to meet the children. The first rays of sunlight passed through the dislocated planks of the woodshed, casting golden stripes on the ground and making the dew sparkle. Ricardo and Angel were not up and the children had not yet arrived; Paolo was impatient! The sharp morning air stung his face, but this was not unpleasant. Nothing unpleasant could happen on such a beautiful day! He started to prance noiselessly around the side of the house.

As he went to the back, he saw a car drive up. He thought it was his new friends. Happily, he ran toward the vehicle.

The driver stopped the motor and a door opened; but instead of the children he was expecting, two men in uniform rushed out. Without a word, they grabbed Paolo and put their hands over his mouth to keep him from shouting. They pushed him inside the car like a bag of wheat.

"Everything is all right now," one of the policemen whispered in his ear. "We're here and you're safe."

Another officer noticed the red mark on Paolo's cheek and shook his head. "This child has been through hell. It was time we got here."

Two other men got out of the front seat of the car. They drew their guns and silently moved toward the house. Paolo moaned under the hand that crushed his mouth. He heard two shots fired and thought his head was exploding.

A few minutes passed; then one of the policemen came running back to the car, panic-stricken. The gun was still in his hand. Blood stained his uniform.

"It wasn't him!" he shouted.

The man who was gagging Paolo removed his hand and opened the car door. Paolo jumped out, a huge knot in his throat.

"We hit a snag!" the policeman went on, all out of breath. "Allegria has disappeared, and Lopez is hurt!"

The men ignored Paolo and rushed over to the house. Alone in the sun, the child could feel the pulsations of the whole universe in his heart. The ground was opening under his feet, the sky was shaking in front of his eyes, and this made everything wobble—everything from the core of the earth to the far end of the immense cosmos.

He went straight to the window of Ricardo's room. And there, on tiptoe, between the half-drawn curtains, he saw the body of the policeman called Lopez. He leaned farther down. A wrinkled hand that was holding an old hunting rifle could be seen near the policeman, and it was not moving. Paolo looked up: the other three policemen were hustling through the doorway of the small room. They appeared distraught and stupidly alive in front of death, in front of the white curtains, the perfumed sheets, the waxed furniture. Paolo turned. The way in front of him was wide open, like a temporary gap between two worlds. On one side of the gap were the police, death, and Ricardo lying on the ground; on the other side were the unknown, solitude, and north. And, perhaps, Angel?

Paolo touched the handle of the knife lightly. Without thinking, he started to run.

He ran faster than he had ever run, as if fear were attached to the soles of his shoes. His temples tensed up, his lower lip trembled.

He did not want to think about what had happened. Confronting the reality of things made his mind go wild; he could not believe that they had killed Ricardo; he refused to believe that Angel had abandoned him in the middle of the night; and he did not want to believe that life was so painfully unfair.

In front of him were the open path, sky, grass, pebbles, fallen branches, misshapen trees, Chile, and somewhere in this direction, his house. He stumbled a few times, grazing the palms of his hands on the rough ground. Now and then he also stopped to calm the fire in his lungs and the pain in his ribs. As he groaned, he remembered the music, the poems, the tears, and the peace gone by. He felt so alone that he could have torn his heart out with his bare hands.

✣

The police car caught up with him half an hour later.

He was standing still, facing what looked like emptiness. The policemen approached him as slowly as pigeon hunters so as not to frighten him. They could see only his back, shaking with spasms. They did not understand. They did not see that Paolo was laughing as he stood there. The policemen did not see the three children who played barefoot in the moss, capering and leapfrogging to amuse their friend. And yet the children were having such fun! It was wonderful to see them, with their Dutch blond hair and their lace clothing swirling in the fresh air.

"No!" Paolo shouted when he felt the hands of the policemen grab him.

Right away, the three children stopped playing. They waved goodbye to Paolo and vanished instantly.

Paolo tried to fight. He brandished Angel's knife above his head, but one of the policemen grabbed his arm. Paolo was not strong enough. His fingers let go of the smooth handle, and the knife fell on a stone, where the blade broke.

"We don't want to harm you," the chief officer declared before ordering his men to take Paolo away.

In the car, the three surviving policemen shifted the body of Officer Lopez to make room for Paolo near the window at the back. The dead man was losing blood on the seat and his head kept falling onto the side of the child, terrifying him.

The policemen never uttered a word.

They did not apologize.

Their small dark eyes were fixed on the bumpy road.

They did not notice that next to them the child was drowning in his sorrow. After all, they considered themselves knights of law and order, fighting evil in the world. It never occurred to them that things were not so simple.

A voice full of static came through the dashboard speaker: Angel Allegria had just been arrested by another squad, twenty kilometers north.

And so it was that the four men mandated by the authorities destroyed the shaky happiness that a child thought was his. They had shown that they were powerful, more powerful than the yellow sweet.

For them, the day was an achievement.

CHAPTER TWENTY-FOUR

PAOLO SAW ANGEL for the last time a few weeks later at the Puerto Natales jail. The windowless room was painted light green and oozed fear, solitude, and boredom.

At first, they were unable to speak. Neither one of them knew words strong enough to express what was in his heart.

The corrections officer finally touched Angel's shoulder. "You don't have much time. Speak up."

Angel gave a start, looking fearfully at the guard from the corner of his eye. In just a few weeks, jail had done its work: the fear of blows had made him obedient; and because his mind was no longer in control of his body, he had given up the fight. Paolo did not recognize the man, once so strong and unwavering, who had carried him for hours along the cliffs.

They looked at each other again, a long time, their throats tight.

"Come on, time's up," said the officer.

Angel leaned slightly toward Paolo as a mother would lean above a crib. It was all over and yet he felt he had not begun.

"Do you remember?" he whispered at last. "When we lived in your house, I asked you to remember what day you were born?"

Paolo nodded. He remembered everything, each moment, each word, each leg of their journey, vividly.

"You answered me it was the day I arrived," Angel went on.

"Time's up!" the guard said again, grabbing Angel's arm firmly.

Angel's hands were handcuffed behind his back and already the guard was pulling him away.

"Do you remember, Paolo?" Angel shouted, his feet slipping on the tiles.

"Yes!" Paolo shouted.

Angel was crying.

"Well, me too!" the murderer yelled. "Me too, I was born that day! I was born the day I saw you! Do you understand, Paolo?"

The guard pulled on the handcuffs and Angel disappeared behind a reinforced door, which closed like a jaw on its prey. Paolo knew that he would never see Angel again. He jumped up, knocking over his chair, and ran to the door.

"I understand!" he shouted behind the door. "Angel! I understand!"

A voice answered, muffled by the thickness of the walls. Were these words expressing sentiments of love? Just in case, Paolo shouted as loudly as he could.

"Me too! Me too!"

And then there was only the clatter of keys, the locking of bolts, the awful grating of jail iron. His hands glued to the door, Paolo did not move. He thought that if he did he would turn to dust, that he would disintegrate like a piece of chalk. He could visualize the walls separating him from Angel. How many of them were there? Dozens, no doubt, each one thicker than the last, green and cold like snakes.

A woman came into the room and put her hand on Paolo's hair.

"Are you all right?" she asked.

Paolo shook his head.

"Do you want to eat something?"

"No, I want my father."

The woman crouched in front of him. She sighed. "Your father is dead, you know."

"Angel."

"Angel is not your father."

"He loves me."

"I don't think so. He has done you a lot of harm."

The woman believed that Paolo was traumatized

because of the years spent with the murderer. She had read papers written by experts in psychiatry that explained how an attachment could develop between victims and their abusers, and how this often formed a binding link. She had read a lot of things, but she knew nothing about the feelings Paolo and Angel shared.

✛

Soon after, the town of Puerto Natales inaugurated its new Court of Justice with much fanfare. It was a very tall, impressive building, with lots of steps leading to a huge entrance guarded on each side by a statue that was half lioness, half woman. The recently elected mayor was dedicating the court to his voters, vowing to uphold his campaign promises of a larger police force and less leniency for criminals.

In an immense marble hall in the center of the building, the mayor was about to unveil a surprise.

"Ladies and gentlemen!" he exclaimed as he got ready to pull on a tarpaulin. "You'll understand the meaning of my mission when you see what I am about to reveal. You'll understand how determined I am to make an example of our city as a sanctuary of security for us and our children."

The mayor felt very sure of himself: what was simpler than setting apart good from evil, good people from bad people, honest people from dishonest ones?

He pulled on the tarpaulin. The cloth fell away like the

sail of a boat that sagged for lack of wind. A chorus of *ohs* erupted from the onlookers.

"This guillotine," explained the mayor, satisfied with the effect it had produced, "has been built entirely in Puerto Natales, with the trees of our forests, felled by our best lumberjacks. Its wood has been cut in one of the city sawmills. Its parts have been assembled in one of our factories. A guillotine one hundred percent Chilean! It is for you! Let it be the symbol of our intransigence!"

The crowd burst into applause.

Ricardo Murga had died at the right moment after all. He would never know what his last tree had been used for, or the unusual metamorphosis it had gone through.

✣

Inside the jail, Angel was awaiting trial.

His cell smelled of urine and mildew. Once a day, he was entitled to a ten-minute walk. The sadness of the place and of his life as a whole weighed on his mind all the time. He could not think. They had laughed at him when he had asked for access to the library, since his file said he was illiterate. No one guessed that he had learned to read just by listening to Paolo's lessons with Luis. No one knew how much the years spent with the child had changed him; and no one would have believed it anyway.

To keep his hands busy, he engraved his name on the walls of his cell with a tiny piece of wire torn from the box spring of his bed. *Angel Allegria. Angel Allegria. Angel Allegria.* It was the only thing he could write, the name that life had given him and that sounded so ironic to his ears.

On his birthday, he started to draw a cake and candles. A fine dust of plaster remained suspended in the air like sparkles, and they stuck to his eyes and brought up tears.

His trial took place the following day.

In the courtroom, he looked for Paolo among the crowd. The child was not there. Angel felt both relieved and hurt, but he hid his grief and sat silently in the box for the accused.

A few people spoke. His entire life was stripped apart, fact after fact, offense after offense, crime after crime, until nothing, or almost nothing, was left untold. At the end of the trial, he was just an empty shell.

Only a few hours later, his sentence was read: Angel Allegria was condemned to death.

He was taken back to his cell, where he lay down on the narrow bed. His life was behind him. The only things he had left were the memories of the years of wind, solitude, and happiness with Paolo. But now that he was far from the child, he feared for him, his health, well-being, and future. And no one was willing to give him any news.

Looking at the ceiling, he wished they would execute him as soon as possible and put an end to the worries churning in his head. He called for a corrections officer.

"I want to die," he said.

The guard laughed. "You're in luck."

"Kill me, then."

The guard shook his head. He explained that convicts on death row were not executed that simply. It would take time. The lawyers, the judge, the clerks had to file a lot of paperwork and go through complicated administrative procedures. It would take weeks, perhaps months. Heads were not savagely cut: it was done by state-of-the-art equipment.

✤

Paolo had been put in the care of a family in Puerto Natales. He attended school and was well fed. He did not cause any problems to the decent foster parents in charge of his education. He was calm. Very calm.

Unknown to everyone, he kept a box under his bed in which he had placed the yellow lucky charm. It had become sticky, flat, and dirty after remaining so long in his pocket. The sweet was the only tangible memory he had of his life with Angel. He had lost all the other gifts: the fox; Delia's painting; Luis's money; the record, which he had left at Ricardo's; and even the knife. All these gifts were like little Tom Thumb's bread crumbs: they had been scattered along the way, only to be gathered up by others—especially the money.

At night, questions plagued his mind.

Where was Luis?

What had become of Ricardo's house?

Were the children still coming to dance on the grass?

Was the lovely lamb of Punta Arenas still alive?

And the Belgian alpinist?

And the nice lady at the bank?

There was no one to answer these questions.

One day Paolo inquired whether he could visit Angel in jail. He was told that it was not possible. Children were not allowed to visit prisoners on death row. Besides, he was not to love this man, this murderer, anymore. It was not normal.

So Paolo shut himself in his room. He did not understand the meaning of all this. He took his head in his hands and waited. By dint of waiting, he hoped his heart would wear out and stop beating. What other way was there to stop loving someone?

✤

A long time passed before Paolo was told that he had come of age. He was now eighteen years old. How people determined his age was a mystery, but it meant that from then on he could do whatever he wished, go wherever he wanted to, and dispose of his life as he pleased.

It was a cold, rainy morning. Paolo walked the streets at random and arrived by chance at the jail. He looked up at the high walls. The sky was pouring down on his bare head, onto the sidewalk and the barbed wire. Paolo realized that he was no longer a child. This thought had a strange effect on him, as if the transformation had happened suddenly, without his being aware of it.

He stopped in front of a shop window facing the jail and looked at his reflection. He was not very tall, but his square shoulders and his unshaven cheeks gave him a manly look. He wondered if Angel would recognize him.

He smiled and crossed the street in a steady stride. In a glass cubicle, an old guard was half asleep.

"I've come for a visit," Paolo said, knocking on the window.

The man opened his eyes slightly.

"What name?" he grumbled.

"Angel Allegria."

"The murderer?"

"Yes."

The old guard rubbed his long neck with a wrinkled and yellow hand. Paolo thought he probably had a sore throat.

"You want to see Angel Allegria?" the guard said again, frowning. "Are you a member of his family?"

"Almost," Paolo said. "I knew him well."

Slowly the old man got up. He brought his face close to the speakerphone.

"You're lucky to be alive," he blurted out. "The others who came across Allegria can't say as much."

Paolo just smiled. He had given up trying to explain that he owed his life to Angel. His life—and much more.

"Can I see him?" he persisted.

"No," the old guard answered. "He's dead. He was executed last year, didn't you know?"

Paolo remained frozen on the sidewalk, the rain

dripping on his head. No, he hadn't known. No one had deemed it necessary to tell him.

"I'm sorry," the old man said as he sat down again. "That's the way it is. Justice was served."

Paolo took a step back. The top of the jail had disappeared under the clouds. He looked again at the old guard, thanked him for the information, and turned on his heels. He did not know what he was going to do with his life, but he had a very definite idea of how to spend his day.

CHAPTER TWENTY-FIVE

NOTHING HAD CHANGED. It was still the same landscape, stony and hostile. From the gravel on the path, the
rocks rising from the ground, the expanse of parched land
crushed by the sky, beaten by the winds, and whipped by the
rains—this torn fragment of Chile where men struggle to
keep standing: this was the birthplace of Paolo.

Having lived in town these many years, Paolo was
shocked by the ruggedness, and could not believe he had
been born here. He had only a vague memory of his
mother: a skinny, bony, and dark woman. She had carried
him in her womb, in her narrow and inhospitable belly.

That was her story. Her heart had probably been composed of the same hardness rocks are made of.

He passed by the ruins of the shed that Luis had so poorly built and quickly abandoned when the first rains had come. Then he saw his house, its low decrepit façade, and its only window, darkened by the closed shutter.

He stopped a moment to catch his breath. Gusts of rain lashed his face. He wondered whether coming back had been the right decision, or if keeping only the dream, the memory of the place alive would have been better. A few steps ahead, the mound of dirt under which his parents were resting seemed untouched. Nothing had grown on top of it, not even weeds. Paolo forced himself to go to the fox's grave, also barren of weeds, then made his way to the door of the house.

When he opened it, he felt a bolt of electricity at the back of his neck. It reminded him of his science class at Puerto Natales high school, and of the frogs that had been electrocuted and yet still looked alive in death.

Inside, the house was cold and dark. Paolo groped his way to the window, opened it, and unlocked the shutter. A draft rushed in and he heard a noise. Turning, he saw dozens of small rectangular envelopes on the table. The wind was blowing them around the room. He closed the window and bent down to pick up the scattered mail. He made a pile of the envelopes and thumbed through them as if they were a pack of playing cards. The room was as he remembered it: the bench, the fireplace, the shelf, and, at the back, the small recess. How had these envelopes arrived here? On each of them was his name, neatly written: Paolo Poloverdo. And his address: The House at the End of Earth, the Last One Before the Sea.

He tore an envelope open at random. Inside was a postcard, a picture of Madrid; on the back had been copied the verses of a poem by Federico García Lorca that Paolo did not take time to read.

The second envelope contained a postcard from Rangoon, Burma. The third a postcard from China. The fourth from Naples. The fifth from Mexico. The sixth from Paris. . . . On the back of each of them, the same person had copied poems written by Paul Éluard, Keats, Aragon, Quevedo, and Jules Supervielle.

Paolo stood near the table, feeling feverish as he emptied the envelopes and let them drop to the ground. When he finished, the ripped envelopes covered his shoes up to his ankles, and it seemed that the whole world rested in a jumble atop the table. A world of colors, of sunsets over the Tagus, of snows blanketing Red Square, of shimmering light over rice paddies, of deserts and dunes, of swarming cities, of overcrowded trains, of Chinese people on bicycles, and of dark oceans.

Dizzy, Paolo went to sit on the bench. Luis had accomplished his mission and it was here, on this table, where blood had been spilled and dried, in this lonely house, that he had made all these cities, all these marvelous countries meet. It was as if this house were the crossroads of all roads, and as if all the words of all the poets of the world had decided to meet under the eyes of a child. Luis had transcribed their songs of love, life, beauty, and rapture, unflinchingly. It was a breathtaking way to ask for forgiveness.

Paolo gathered the cards in his arms and rested his cheek on them. At that moment, the door opened.

Paolo uttered a cry and shot up.

"Who's there?" a voice asked.

"It's me," Paolo answered cautiously.

He saw a woman walk in. A woman covered by a large rain cape.

"You are . . . Paolo Poloverdo?" she asked.

"Yes."

"So you're back?"

Paolo looked at her: she was young, her cheeks were very red, locks of wet hair were glued to her forehead. He wondered what to answer. Was he back for good, or only for a while? He looked at her hands and noticed a small piece of paper showing under the folds of her cape.

"I will light a fire," he said. "It is cold."

He got up and went to the recess. Just as he hoped, there was still a good amount of dry wood. When he came back to the room, the young woman had not moved. She watched him get busy in front of the fireplace, and she smiled when the logs started to burn.

"I was wondering whether you really existed," she said.

"And?"

"It seems that you do."

Paolo picked up the fire iron and poked at the blaze. Lots of sparks went up the chimney. The young woman came near him.

"Here. This arrived yesterday."

It was the most recent card from Luis. Paolo opened it. It had come from Valparaiso. And this time, no poem was written on the back. Paolo smiled.

"Good news?" the young woman asked.

"Someone wishing me happy birthday."

"Is it your birthday?"

"Apparently."

The young woman sat near Paolo.

"Happy birthday," she whispered.

She removed her cape. Underneath, she wore the uniform of the Chilean post office.

EPILOGUE

UNDER THE YOUNG woman's postal uniform, Paolo discovered many wonderful things.

Terusa was twenty-five years old, was very patient, had a marvelous laugh and a rusty bicycle that grated and rang joyously on the stones of the path.

✤

On a sunny morning, Paolo made a decision. He dragged the table over the uneven slabs of the floor and pulled it outside. In the clear spring light, one could still notice the red stains, the traces of blood in the thick grooves of the wood.

Paolo ran into the house, rummaged feverishly inside the recess, then came out with his father's ax. He was perspiring a little and was out of breath, but he was determined. He raised the ax above his head.

The blade came tumbling down on the table and drove into it, deeply.

By the fifth blow, the table split in two, like an overripe fruit.

By the seventh blow, the legs flew into pieces.

It was warm. Paolo drank a gulp of water directly from the bucket.

After an hour's work, the table was in bits. Paolo kept the drawer because there was no other place to put the corkscrew and forks. He looked at his work. He felt better.

Around him, the light was changing, subject to the tantrums of the winds and the high clouds. He went inside to put away the ax, and brought out a shovel.

As he approached the mound of dry dirt, he remembered the dark night when he had held the storm lantern to provide Angel with light. It had been the night of the first soup. It seemed to him it had happened a century ago.

He dug a hole next to the fox's grave. Then he put the pieces of the table in a wheelbarrow, pushed the wheelbarrow over the stones, and threw its contents into the hole. His throat was as tight as if he were at a funeral.

Just then, he heard the jingle of Terusa's bicycle coming up the path and turned around. She looked happy and radiant, her empty mailbag flying behind her. Paolo let go of the shovel.

"What are you doing?" Terusa asked as she got off her bicycle near the hole.

"I'm going to make a new table," Paolo answered.

Terusa leaned down. She looked at the pieces of wood scattered at the bottom of the hole. It seemed strange, but she loved Paolo as he was, quirks and all.

"Good," she said. "In the meantime, we'll eat on the floor."

She went to park her bicycle. Paolo took his shovel again and filled the hole. When he finished, he packed the dirt down a bit. He was thinking of Angel, and of Angel's large hands. Then Terusa called to him.

Lunch was ready.

❖

Some time later, Luis came to visit. He had just buried his father in Valparaiso, on one of the slopes overlooking the bay. It was the reason he had come back to Chile, for the father whom he had not seen for so many years, and who had died alone after having dispersed children, wives, and bottles of wine all around the globe.

He told Paolo how much he had missed the love of his father and how big a void this was in his life, even today.

Delia, then other women, had fallen into this void, this emptiness. They had passed through it; nothing had stopped their fall. This was why he had come back to Chile alone.

"The day of the funeral, I saw my brother and sisters again," he told Paolo and Terusa. "My sisters have put on weight. They have had children and I think that they are bored to death. As for my brother, the one who dreamed of becoming an actor, well . . ." Luis concealed a smile behind his hand. ". . . well, he has really become an actor! I did not know it because I don't watch TV, but there was a good number of fans waiting for him at the gate of the cemetery to get his autograph."

"Come in," Paolo said. "You must be thirsty."

Luis was surprised to see the changes that Paolo had made in the house.

"A new table?" he said.

"The other one was dead," Paolo answered.

"This one is very beautiful," Luis admitted.

He was also very impressed by the bookshelves Paolo had built. As a token, he placed a book there, the one that told of storms, of sailors thrown back to shore, the book in which Paolo had heard the voice of poets for the first time.

"Now I know all the words," Paolo murmured, stroking the cover.

Luis sighed. He went around the room, examining the postcards that hung on the walls. It was as if his life had been preserved in a museum. The memories were fading away, feelings were less acute, everything was taking its real place again; and the world, the countries he had visited, would never be worth the time he had spent in this lonely house, where he had fought the winds and the silent rages of Angel, the fox, the snakes, or the peaceful moments spent smoking at sunset. Paolo was the owner of something invaluable: a spot on this earth where he was truly at home, and where a person feels at one with the universe because of its roughness.

Before he left, Luis unloaded several cases of wine from his car—wine he had inherited from his father. Chilean, French, Spanish, Italian wines, each one more delicious than the last.

"Where are you going next?" Paolo asked him.

Luis smiled. "I've never known where I was going."

He wanted to add something but changed his mind. Maybe he had wanted to talk about Angel; whatever it was, Paolo was grateful that he kept silent.

"I'm sorry," Luis whispered nevertheless, before he rushed to his car.

He drove off and disappeared at the end of the path, waving goodbye from the window.

❖

Paolo never went back to Ricardo Murga's house, but each time he had to enter the forest, he thought of Ricardo and remembered when he and Angel had first heard the lumberjack's ax striking the wood. In the evenings, he got in the habit of lighting a lot of candles on the table in memory of this man and his ghosts.

Some days, he would go for a solitary walk to the spot where the ground breaks and the sea begins. Standing there in silence, he faced the uproar of the icy waters and wondered time and time again about the reasons that pushed him to live. He never found an answer. To be born and alive was the only feeling that persisted, as inescapable and as real as a rock, in spite of everything. And ultimately this feeling satisfied him.

❖

From time to time, a stranger showed up on the rocky path. Most often it was a scientist, a geologist with a box of stones, or an astronomer in quest of a dark night. Sometimes it was a poet trying to decipher the Chilean soul. Other times it was simply an adventurer looking for spots yet undiscovered and far from the beaten path.

Paolo welcomed them, his door wide open. He laughed at their surprise when they discovered the interior of the house. The bookshelves, rugs, candles, postcards, clean curtains . . . Paolo would pour a glass of wine from the "Secunda Reserve" for his guests, and he enjoyed making them chat. They brought him news of the world. The reports floated up in the room like bubbles, where they burst upon reaching the ceiling. Wars, famines, revolutions, epidemics, woes of the financial market, strikes, accidents, royal weddings, and automobile races reached the ceiling of the small house at the end of the earth, and lost a little of their importance there.

At the end of the evening, the guests would listen quietly to the howling of the wind behind the window and drink the wine as their eyes skimmed over the spines of the books on the shelves.

❖

Years went by.

❖

Later, Terusa gave birth to a child, a girl.

Paolo suggested they name her Angelina. Terusa saw only wings and a halo in the name. She accepted it without hesitation.

AUTHOR'S NOTE

In Chile, the death penalty was given for the last time in 1985, and was officially abolished in 2001.

About the Author

Anne-Laure Bondoux was born near Paris in 1971. She has written several novels for young people in varied genres and has received numerous literary prizes in her native France. Her previous novels published in the United States are *The Destiny of Linus Hoppe* and its companion, *The Second Life of Linus Hoppe*. *The Killer's Tears* was awarded France's prestigious Prix Sorcières.